Fanny and the Monsters

Fanny came round a corner, and found herself looking across a small stretch of water at an island. The island was covered with trees and bushes, and there among the trees and bushes . . .

. . . There among the trees and bushes – oh marvel of marvels! – was the most enormous, terrifying, utterly unexpected creature, rearing up on its hindlegs, rust red in colour, and apparently chewing the leaves off a chestnut tree.

PENELOPE LIVELY

Fanny and the Monsters

Illustrated by
JOHN LAWRENCE

MAMMOTH

First published in Great Britain 1983
by William Heinemann Ltd
Published 1991 by Mammoth
an imprint of Mandarin Paperbacks
Michelin House, 81 Fulham Road, London SW3 6RB
Reprinted 1992

Mandarin is an imprint of Reed Consumer Books Ltd

First published as three separate volumes
Fanny's Sister © 1976
Fanny and the Monsters © 1979
Fanny and the Battle of Potter's Piece © 1980
Illustrations © John Lawrence 1976, 1979, 1980

ISBN 0 7497 0600 7

A CIP catalogue record for this title
is available from the British Library

Printed in Great Britain
by Cox & Wyman Ltd, Reading, Berkshire

Contents

To Sophie and Emma

Fanny's Sister

Fanny dreamed that a cat was mewing outside her door. Be quiet, she said to it crossly, in her sleep, be quiet or you'll wake me up. The dream dissolved and she woke, warmly buried in her own bed, with a bright crack of light down the middle of the curtains telling her that it was morning. Outside, the milkman's pony clopped along the road, and a voice (Cook's, it must be, or Nellie the kitchen-maid perhaps) called out to him from the back door.

And something was mewing. But not a cat. Fanny sat bolt upright in bed, and listened. She knew that noise. It was the noise that started up afresh, next door in the nursery, as regularly, it seemed to Fanny, as Christmas and Easter and birthdays. Last year when she was eight and the year before when she was seven and the year before . . . well, nearly every year anyway, because Fanny was the eldest and then there were Albert and Emma and Harriet and Charles and Jane and Susan.

It was the noise of a new baby. A brand new, just-born baby. In there, thought Fanny, sitting up in bed freezing in her flannel nightie, and glaring at the closed door between the night-nursery and the day-nursery, in there, tucked up in the cradle, was a new baby, red of face and loud of voice. Mamma, who had

9

been not-very-well for weeks and weeks so that you must not jump and shout on the stairs, would be lying pale and smiling in the big bed and presently Fanny and Albert and all the others would be taken in one by one to say good morning in hushed voices and give her one quiet and gentle kiss before they went away again. And in the nursery there would be that mewing noise, night and day, with Nurse all cross and busy at the washing steaming in front of the fire, and no time for stories after tea. Her huge, white-aproned lap would be occupied by the new baby, as it had been occupied by last-year's baby (Susan) and the baby of the year before that and the year before that. Once upon a time, a long time ago, in a time that seemed all golden and glorious, like pictures of Heaven in Fanny's Bible, that lap had been Fanny's place. There she had sat, and listened to stories and had squares of hot buttered toast popped into her mouth. And then there had come Albert and the lap had been only partly hers, and then Emma and it was no longer hers at all and presently she found herself pushed upwards into the schoolroom, to Miss Purser with her rabbity teeth and her ruler that tapped your knuckles if you did not pay attention, and her horrible, horrible sums.

I hate babies, said Fanny to the picture of an angel on the wall at the foot of her bed, and the angel, its halo exploding into a fiery sky, stared disapprovingly back, because nice little girls do not hate anything, least of all their dear little brothers and sisters.

The door opened. The hump of bedclothes in the

next bed that was Emma sat up and said she was hungry for breakfast.

"All in good time," said Nurse. She drew the curtains and light came into the room, and a blackbird's song, and the church bells ringing. It must be Sunday, thought Fanny, and alongside the crossness that the mewing noise had brought came a further crossness at the thought of Sunday. Sunday meant church, and learning by heart a passage from the Bible, and no noisy games, and more church, and repeating the passage from the Bible to Papa in his study. I hate Sundays, said Fanny to the angel, and the angel raised its eyes to the fiery sky in horror and disbelief.

Now everybody was awake. Susan began to cry and Nurse picked her up and started to dress her. "Come along now, Fanny," she said, "up you get. Don't you want to see what a nice surprise there is for you in the nursery?"

No, said Fanny silently.

"I know," said Albert, "there is a new baby. The new baby has come. Is it a boy or a girl?"

"A lovely little girl," said Nurse. She put Susan on the floor to crawl around and set about brushing Harriet's hair, briskly, taking no notice of Harriet's loud protesting noises. "A little sister for you."

"Hurry!" said Emma, and Albert groaned theatrically until Nurse snapped at him to be quiet.

"Did God send the new baby?" said Harriet, wriggling under the hairbrush, and Nurse said yes, God sent the new baby and in church today they must all say thank you to Him. "What's the matter with you, Fanny?" she went on, whipping clothes out of drawers. "Get up and put on your Sunday dress."

"I feel ill," said Fanny. "I have . . . I have a stomach-ache. And my throat is sore. And my legs hurt," she added. If you were going to do a thing you might as well do it properly. Nurse herself said that, almost every day.

"Let me see your tongue," said Nurse. And then, "Get up this minute. I never heard such nonsense."

Fanny got up, scowling, and scowled her way into her tight, stiff Sunday dress and boots and then into the nursery where Sukie the nursery maid was ladling porridge into bowls. In the cradle by the fire the new baby mewed and Nurse picked it up and talked to it and then took it away upstairs to Mamma. Fanny burned her tongue on her porridge and kicked Albert under the table, half by accident and half on purpose, so that Albert kicked back and there was a fight, and when Nurse returned Albert was sent to stand in one corner of the room and Fanny in the other.

"Birds in their little nests agree," said Nurse. "You can stop there now, the pair of you, till I say." And Fanny, staring sullenly at the wallpaper, thought that Nurse couldn't know all that much about birds. What about baby cuckoos, she thought? They push all the other little birds out so that there's only them left. Clever cuckoos, she said to herself, and behind her, at the table, last year's baby (Susan) spattered her breakfast on the floor and howled.

Breakfast ended. Fanny and Albert were released from their corners. Nurse scolded them again and said that badly-behaved children would not be allowed to go upstairs before church and see their Mamma. Then the Old Children (Fanny, Albert and Emma) were sent to the schoolroom to write out the Sunday text and learn it by heart to recite to Papa while the Young Children (all the rest) were taken off by Sukie to be cleaned and put into outdoor clothes and packed into the donkey-cart for an airing. Fanny wished, and not for the first time, that she was still one of the Young Children.

In the schoolroom, a bluebottle, trapped like Fanny, buzzed fretfully against the window. Fanny opened her exercise book and wrote the date at the top of a clean page: Sunday 6 September 1865. In the middle of the green baize tablecloth was a sheet of paper on which Papa had written in his neat sloping handwriting the verses from the Bible that they were to copy out and learn. Fanny began to write, in her not-so-neat writing ". . . And God said unto them, Be fruitful, and multiply, and replenish the earth." It was

all about Adam and Eve, this bit. God was telling them what they were to do and what they weren't to do. Fanny knew what mulitply meant, because of Miss Purser and her horrible sums. That is what we are doing, too, she thought, being fruitful and multiplying, because there is a new baby every year. God must think we are a nice obedient family. And she looked balefully out of the window down into the street outside the house, where she could see Hobbs the groom standing beside the donkey cart, holding the donkey while the Young Children were loaded into the cart, two at each side. They all looked happy and excited and Fanny, watching them, remembered what it used to feel like jogging down the lanes, holding on to the wooden sides of the donkey cart with both hands, while Nurse led the donkey and the donkey's furry ears twitched against the flies. It's not fair, thought Fanny in a rage, it just isn't fair.

Dust spun in a shaft of sunshine. Albert sighed and grunted as he wrote, the tip of his tongue sticking out between his teeth. Emma ground her boots maddeningly upon the leg of her chair and muttered as she learned by heart. Fanny said to herself, over and over again, "And God saw everything he had made, and behold it was very good," and thought gloomily that she would never know this to say to Papa tonight. She would stammer and stutter and stop and Papa would be displeased and it would not be good at all.

At last Nurse came to fetch them to get ready for church. When they were washed and brushed they went down into the hall to wait for Papa to come from his study and take them to see Mamma. Fanny, her hands clasped inside her fur muff (she liked her Sunday muff, it was the only thing that was agreeable about Sundays) heard the door open on the floor above and his footsteps coming down the stairs, and then there was his large, black figure above her, complete with shiny black Sunday hat, and the gold watch-chain stretched across his waistcoat. When she was very young she had longed to pull that watch-chain but had never dared because Papa was not the kind of person to whom you could ever, ever do such a thing. Fanny loved her father, and she thought him extremely grand and important, but he seemed somehow very far away, even though she lived in the same house with him and always had done. Loving him was more like loving God or the Queen than loving, for instance, Nurse, or Jupiter the sheepdog or the donkey or even Mamma, who was also grand and a little far away but not nearly so far away as Papa.

Mamma, this morning, lay in bed in the big up-stairs bedroom like a piece of precious china cocooned in tissue paper. She smiled and kissed each of them and asked what they thought of their new little sister. Emma said that she was nice and Albert said that she was nice but it was a pity she had not been a boy.

"Come now, Fanny," said Papa, "have you lost your tongue? What do you think?"

"She makes a lot of noise," said Fanny in a sullen voice, and Mamma and Papa both laughed and said

that all babies cry and that was perfectly natural. Outside, the church bells were ringing, which made Papa take his watch from his waistcoat pocket and say that it was time to go.

Walking to church, Fanny forgot her irritation about the new baby. There was a dog-fight at the end of their street, which was exciting and interesting, and blackberries to pick in the hedge along the lane (quickly, behind Papa's back, cramming them into her mouth before he could see) and her best enemy, Clara Binns the doctor's daughter, outside the church gates. Fanny and Clara stuck out their tongues at each other, as far as they would go, while Papa removed his hat to Mrs Binns and Mrs Binns enquired after Mamma and sent effusive messages of congratulations and affection.

"Shall I say thank you to God for the new baby, Papa?" said Emma, and Papa smiled and patted Emma's head and said yes, that would be very nice. And all Fanny's crossness came flowing back.

Kneeling in their pew, Fanny stared through a crack in her fingers at the Sunday bonnet of Mrs Binns in front of her (a new bonnet, with much in the way of ribbons and flowers and fruit, a ridiculous bonnet, in Fanny's opinion) and thought about God. She always imagined that God, if one ever saw him, would look rather like Papa, but in long flowing robes, like people in the Bible, and even sterner. She began to pray. First she thought of all the things she had done wrong since last Sunday and said she was sorry about them. I am sorry, she said silently, that I pinched Emma (but it was because she spoiled my book so I hope she is saying she is sorry to You, too) and I am sorry I wouldn't eat my rice-pudding (but You created rice-pudding which is a pity and if You had not I wouldn't have to eat it) and I am sorry I was rude to Nurse. She paused to try to remember if there was anything she had left out, as God would know anyway, since He was supposed to know everything. And anything that I have forgotten, she added. And please make me good. She always asked this. And it seemed to her that God was not being very successful. But perhaps in her case it was a great deal more difficult than in most and was just taking longer.

A fly settled on the bunch of cherries at the side of Mrs Binns' bonnet, apparently deceived by their natural appearance. Fanny watched it with interest until it flew away, and the cherries made her think of cherry tart. Her mouth watered. She dearly loved cherry tart. Cherry tart with a great deal of clotted cream. And it had not appeared upon the dinner table for a very long time now. Months and months. Years, even. Please, said Fanny to God, please may we have cherry tart for dinner today. From time to time she asked God for small things like this. She had never asked for anything large, because she did not feel that she really deserved it, but small things, such as cherry tarts and a day with no sums to do, she felt could not be objected to. So far, God had never obliged (except just once, over a fine day for her birthday) and she assumed this was because she was so wicked. Cherry tart *and* clotted cream, she prayed. And thank you for sending the new baby, she added, unwillingly. Thank You for sending it even though I didn't ask for it and in fact I wish You would take it back again.

There was a creaking and rustling as the Vicar took his place and everyone stood up to sing the first hymn.

"Alleluia! Alleluia!" sang Fanny lustily, glad to get up off her knees, and in a sudden fit of well-being she nudged Albert, who nudged her back until they were both quelled by a glance from Papa. Fanny put on her most virtuous expression and gazed intently at Mr Chubb, the Vicar, as though she were drinking in his every word. Mr Chubb, she knew, could not see her, as he wore the thickest spectacles she had ever seen on anyone and was famous for never recognising people. He had much offended her Mamma once by mistaking her for Mrs Hancock the grocer's wife. Mamma was very much grander than a grocer's wife.

"Amen," sang Fanny loudly, and the Sunday service unrolled, as familiar in its progress as the rising and setting of the sun, until the Vicar pronounced the blessing and everybody filed out into the churchyard to bow and remove hats to one another.

They went home. Papa was in a most genial mood and allowed them to stop for a few minutes to throw stones into the village pond, and made no comment when Albert climbed upon the stone wall beside the lane and walked along it. Fanny wished that she could follow him but knew that what was allowed—at a pinch—to boys was certainly not allowed to a girl wearing her best Sunday dress and coat. She wished, also, and that too not for the first time, that she was a boy.

At home, the Young Children were just being unloaded from the donkey cart, at the end of their outing. Fanny hugged the donkey and the donkey, who never showed its feelings, except for a general impression of gloom and suffering, stood in resignation, its ears drooping, while she buried her face in the thick dusty fur of its neck.

The Young Children were taken up to the nursery while Fanny, Albert and Emma went with Papa into the dining room for Sunday dinner. One of the only things in favour of being an Older Child, Fanny considered, was that you were allowed into the dining room for Sunday dinner with the grown-ups. Not only did this make you feel interesting and important (even if you did have to pay more than usual attention to good manners), but the food was better. There was no tapioca or semolina, but things like roast beef and Yorkshire pudding. Fanny licked her lips in happy anticipation as she sat down in her place, hands neatly in her lap, lowered her head while Papa said Grace, and raised it again as he picked up the carving knife to sharpen it. There was the most exquisite smell of roast lamb, and, as the green baize door to the kitchen swung to and fro behind Mary the parlourmaid, gusts of something else delicious that she could not for the moment recognize.

They ate. Papa asked them questions about what they had learned in the schoolroom with Miss Purser this week. He was still in a very good humour and only once told Albert to sit up straight and not speak with his mouth full. Fanny, agreeably stuffed with roast lamb, forgot most of her troubles, such as Miss Purser's sums and that passage from the Bible that she would certainly not be able to recite this evening, and chatted to Papa about one thing and another. The roast lamb was taken away to the kitchen and Papa asked Mary to bring in the next course.

"Well, now," said Papa, removing the cover from a dish to release another gust of that pleasant smell that Fanny could not quite place, "what has Cook made for us today?" and his knife hovered over a golden and shining pastry surface. He cut a triangle from the pastry and laid it upon one of the plates in front of him. "Ah! A cherry tart. Cherries and clotted cream. Fanny, will you have a helping of tart?"

Fanny stared at the tart and her eyes grew round with amazement. Cherry tart? Cherry tart *and* clotted

cream? Was she hearing and seeing correctly? But yes, there indeed was the beautiful rosy gleam of cherries steaming beneath the pastry in a bath of thick sweet juice, and there indeed was the silver bowl piled high with yellow clotted cream, being placed by Mary at this very moment in the middle of the table. She had prayed for cherry tart, and lo! cherry tart had been granted to her.

Thank You, said Fanny fervently and silently, and held out her plate to Papa. And at the very same moment a thought struck her, with such suddenness and such effect that the plate quavered in her hand and would have dropped upon the table if Papa had not snatched it from her.

She had asked God for cherry tart. And then she had thanked Him for the new baby and wished that He would take it back again.

And He had granted the first part of her request.

"No!" said Fanny, out loud, in panic, "No! I didn't mean it. Please don't! I didn't really mean it at all!"

"Fanny!" said Papa crossly. "Whatever is the matter with you? Kindly pay attention to what you are doing. And what are you talking about? You didn't mean what?" He handed her plate back to her, piled high with glistening cherries, golden pastry and cream.

"Nothing," said Fanny, and hung her head over the cherries. She stuck her spoon into them, and took a mouthful, and the cherries tasted of nothing at all because her head was filled with a terrible picture of the new baby being swept up to Heaven, naked, with a little pair of wings on its back, like cherubs in the

Bible. She put her spoon down again and stared miserably at the table. Everybody else ate their tart and said they would like a second helping.

"Fanny!" said Papa sternly. "Mary is waiting to clear the plates. Eat up your pudding at once, please."

Fanny took another mouthful, and thought that she might be sick. The cherries were horribly sticky and sweet (how could she ever have liked them?) and the cream full of nasty lumps. With tears in her eyes she crammed spoonful after spoonful into her mouth. Albert and Emma sat staring at her in surprise while Papa, tall and black-clothed and awesome, gazed at the window as though she were not there. Dining room manners did not allow that food should be left uneaten on a plate. Neither, for that matter, did nursery manners, but in the nursery there was the ever open mouth of Sam, the nursery dog, beneath the table.

At last the plate was empty. Papa said Grace again and the children were free to go.

"What's the matter?" whispered Albert on the stairs. "Have you got a stomach-ache?" and Fanny scowled at him and rushed on alone up to the nursery, her heart thumping in horrified anticipation of what she might find. Or rather, not find.

She burst into the nursery, scarlet-faced. There was Nurse seated beside the fire, a goffering-iron in her hand and one of Susan's frilled caps upon her knee. And there was the cradle beside her, empty.

"Where's the baby gone?" cried Fanny in anguish. "What has happened to the baby?"

"No need to shout like that, Fanny," said Nurse calmly. "Where do you think the baby would have gone, child? Up to your Mamma, of course."

Fanny stood still in the middle of the nursery carpet. She stared suspiciously at Nurse (who went on goffering, so that the room was filled with the familiar nursery smell of scorched linen) and said, "I want to see it. Her. Now."

"For gracious' sake!" said Nurse irritably. "What's the matter with you? This morning you hadn't the time for so much as a look at her. Anyone would have thought you weren't best pleased to have a new little sister. You'll see her again all in good time, when Sukie brings her down again."

And, sure enough, in a few minutes there was Sukie with the baby in her arms, crooning at her as she popped her back into the cradle again, where the baby instantly set up a determined wail. Her voice, Fanny noticed, had gained strength even since this morning. Her face seemed even redder, too, and her tiny fists waved about even more vigorously. She was very ugly.

"No need to hang over her like that," said Nurse. "Go off and play now."

But Fanny could not. How could she go and play when any minute . . . When any minute she did not know quite what might happen? She sat miserably beside the cradle and in the cradle the baby howled and Nurse ironed and goffered and sewed and outside in the garden Albert and Emma played quiet Sunday games.

Presently the baby stopped crying and Fanny leapt

anxiously to her feet to gaze into the cradle.

"She's not breathing."

"Of course she's breathing," said Nurse crossly. "Leave her be, child. Do you want to wake her up?" She held the iron close to her cheek to test the heat, and her cheek glowed red in the firelight. It was almost dark now. The gas-lamps hissed quietly to themselves on the four walls of the nursery. Sukie drew the curtains. The baby woke up and waved its fists around and when Fanny loooked into the cradle it suddenly opened its eyes and squinted at her. It had blue eyes, like Mamma and like herself, and despite its red, wrinkled face and bald little head there was a look about it—her—of Mamma. I look like Mamma, thought Fanny, everybody says so. So this baby looks like me.

The baby gave a great sigh, just like a real person, and went to sleep again. "Dear little soul," said Nurse, rocking the cradle with her foot. A proper little angel," and Fanny's heart sank still further. Oh, she thought, in horror, what am I to do?

"Nurse," she said, "if you make a prayer, in church, can you take it back again later? If it was a prayer you didn't mean."

"Certainly not," said Nurse. "I never heard of such a thing."

"Never?"

"And that's no kind of talk for a Sunday. Nor any other day. Get on now and do your neeedlework before tea."

I'll take the baby and hide it, thought Fanny reck-

lessly. And even as she thought she knew that it was
no good. Where could you hide a howling, wriggling
baby? And what, in any case, would be the point of
hiding something from God, who knows everything?

And in gloom and despair, as Sunday afternoon
inched onward into Sunday evening, Fanny decided to
run away. I'll run away, she thought, with tears prick-
ing her eyes, I'll run away and then at least they'll
know I felt bad about it. And I won't ever know what
happened, added a small, guilty voice inside her head
—I won't be here so I won't ever know what happened
to the baby. I'll run away and be a servant, like Nellie
the kitchen-maid, and Papa and Mamma will never

see me again but just think sad thoughts about me. It did occur to her that, if the baby was indeed going to be whisked off to Heaven, it would not be much help to her Papa and Mamma to find that she had disappeared as well, but that problem just confused her. I've got to run away, she thought, there isn't anything else I can do. People in story-books frequently ran away when things got too difficult, and Fanny could see why, now.

She slipped out of the room. Nurse and Sukie were busy; Albert and Emma had come in from the garden and were having an argument. At least two of the Young Children were crying. Nobody saw her go. She put on her Sunday coat and hat and went out of the front door and into the street. It was not until she reached the corner that she realized she had not thought at all about where she was going, except that she was going to find work as a kitchen-maid. Nellie the kitchen-maid at home was not much older than Fanny, and certainly no bigger or stronger. Somebody will want me, thought Fanny dolefully, everybody needs a kitchen-maid. But who? And who, moreover, she realized with alarm, was there in the neighbourhood who did not know her, at least by sight? Everybody in their street knew her, in the big houses that were likely to have room for a kitchen-maid. And nearly everybody in most of the streets round about.

She stood on the corner, under the gas-lamp, feeling very lonely and dejected. It was raining, and she had never before been out in the streets in the darkness by herself. The big houses stared coldly at her through their curtained windows, shutting her out. We have plenty of kitchen-maids already, they seemed to say, be off with you. Fanny began to feel tearful again, and, just as her courage was about to leave her altogether, the church clock struck, and with its striking came inspiration. The Vicarage! The Vicarage, sprawling in its big, gloomy garden beside the church, was quite the biggest house in the place. The Vicar must need kitchen-maids by the dozen. And, best of all, there was very little chance that the Vicar, with his huge thick spectacles and weak blue eyes that could mistake Mamma for stout Mrs Hancock the grocer's wife, would recognize her. To the Vicarage she would go.

The driveway to the front door of the Vicarage, black with bushes and trees behind which anything might lurk, terrified her. She almost ran the last few steps and snatched at the bell-rope as though at a life-belt. Far away, in the depths of the Vicarage, the bell rang, and presently, while Fanny quivered outside the door, footsteps came shuffling down long passages.

The door opened, not very far. Fanny had expected a servant, but there, somewhere a long way above her, for he was a tall man, as well as vastly fat, was the Vicar. Peering down at her through those spectacles.

"Yes?" said Mr Chubb.

Fanny was seized with confusion, and became speechless. She gazed at Mr Chubb and Mr Chubb peered back, with little blue eyes that were perhaps not quite so vague and misty as Fanny had remembered.

"Yes?" he said again.

"Please," said Fanny in a rush, "I've come to be a

kitchen-maid. Please will you have me for your kitchen-maid. I'll work very hard," she added, "I'll work all day and I'll be very good. I'm very strong. And I don't want any money at all," she added as an afterthought.

Mr Chubb hitched his glasses higher on his nose and stared at her. "You'd better come in," he said. He opened the door wider for Fanny to come into the hall, and closed it behind her. In the gaslight he peered at her again, harder, and said at last, "Don't I know you, little girl?"

"No," said Fanny firmly.

"You don't live near here?"

"No," said Fanny. And then she said, "I live in Edinburgh." She said this partly because she knew Edinburgh was a long way away and partly because it was one of the only places she knew of, because her aunt lived there.

"Hmmn," said Mr Chubb. He seemed to be study-ing Fanny's Sunday coat and hat with some interest, and it occurred to Fanny that she was rather grandly dressed for a kitchen-maid. Her everyday clothes would not have been much better, though. She gave the Vicar a faint, hopeful smile.

"Hmmn," he said again. And then, "If you've travelled all the way from Edinburgh I would think you must be cold. You had better come into my study by the fire."

As Fanny followed him into a big room, with books all the way up the walls from top to bottom, he looked back at her over his shoulder and said, "You will have had a long journey, then?"

"Two hours," said Fanny with a little more confidence. She knew that it took about two hours to go from their town to London, and supposed Edinburgh must be quite as far.

"Fancy that," said Mr Chubb thoughtfully. He gave the fire a poke and sat down in an armchair. "Take your coat off and sit down."

They sat and looked at each other. Fanny's gaze wavered before Mr Chubb's blue eyes—really rather sharp blue eyes, she now saw—and she looked away in confusion.

"And what," said Mr Chubb, "makes you think I am in need of a kitchen-maid?"

"This is a very big house," said Fanny timidly. "There must be a lot of work to be done."

"Indeed there is," said Mr Chubb "Indeed there is." He lit his pipe and puffed out a great deal of evil-smelling smoke, through which he and Fanny observed each other.

"And for how long were you in your last position?" said Mr Chubb.

"I beg your pardon?" said Fanny, not understanding at all.

"For how long did you work at the last house where you were employed?"

"Quite a long time," said Fanny, after a little thought.

"Ah," said Mr Chubb, with another gust of smoke. "Your mistress would have been a Scottish lady, I take it?"

"Not particularly," said Fanny with caution.

"Indeed?" said Mr Chubb. "You surprise me. Ladies in Edinburgh are inclined to be Scottish."

Something, Fanny realized, was going wrong with this conversation. "I expect she was sometimes," she said doubtfully.

There was a silence, during which the Vicar heaved and grunted and his pipe bubbled like a stew on the stove. He appeared to be deep in thought. "Well," he said at last. "If you are to be my kitchen-maid you had better set about your duties. Cook is visiting her sister so you will have the kitchen to yourself."

Fanny trotted behind him down what seemed a great many dark cold corridors until they reached the kitchen. She looked around her in dismay, not being familiar with the insides of kitchens (at home the children were always chivvied away by Cook). Mr Chubb had turned to go out of the door.

"What shall I do?" said Fanny.

Mr Chubb looked down at her through those thick spectacles. "Come now, my dear," he said, "I surely do not have to tell you that, if you are an experienced kitchen-maid." He looked beyond Fanny into the ill-lit scullery beyond the kitchen. "No doubt the dishes require washing."

The Vicar's footsteps grew fainter and fainter in the corridor. Fanny found a grubby apron and tied it round her waist. It would not do to soil her Sunday dress, Mamma would be most displeased (but of course she was not going to see Mamma again, so that did not really matter: two large tears welled up at this thought). She poured some water from a jug into a basin and took the first plate from what appeared to be a small mountain of dirty greasy crockery upon the scullery table.

Ten miserable minutes later   though it seemed much longer than that—Fanny had washed, after a fashion, three plates and a jug, and a great many tears had plopped down into the basin in front of her. Her feet were cold and her back ached. Also, she was hungry, and remembered that she had had no tea. Never before in all her nine years had she gone without her tea. More tears of self-pity trickled into the dirty water, checked

35

only for a moment as the new and uncomfortable thought struck her that Nellie the kitchen-maid at home must be doing this now too, and not just now but yesterday and tomorrow and every other day. Poor Nellie, thought Fanny. And poor me too.

As she reached for another plate the kitchen door opened behind her.

"Ah," said Mr Chubb. "You are making good progress, I see." And then "Tut, tut—you have let the stove go out."

Fanny looked in alarm at the great black kitchen range. Ranges, she knew, ate coal. But where did one find coal? And how did one feed that vast, baleful object?

"You will find the coal cellar beyond the back door," said Mr Chubb.

Fanny picked up the coal scuttle and struggled with it to the back door. She filled the scuttle with coal and then found that it was too heavy to carry, so she had to take half of the coal out again. When she got back into the kitchen Mr Chubb, with much wheezing and grunting, was re-lighting the stove with paper and sticks.

"Thank you," said Fanny humbly.

"It seemed to me," said Mr Chubb, "that you are as ill-acquainted with kitchen ranges as I am myself." He peered up at her, over the top of his spectacles this time.

Fanny blushed. The Vicar was turning out to be not at all the kind of person she had expected. And,

furthermore, she had an uncomfortable feeling that he was not taking her absolutely seriously. Could it be that he did not believe her? That, in fact, he had seen straight through her and out the other side, as it were, with those short-sighted blue eyes of his?

"I was merely," Mr Chubb went on, heaving himself to his feet again as the range produced a satisfactory gout of flame within, "I was merely trying to save us both from the wrath of Cook, which is second only to the wrath of God."

Fanny was startled. This sounded suspiciously like some kind of joke, though not the kind of joke Papa ever made. Papa never made jokes about God. But perhaps it was a different matter for Vicars.

"What would Cook do?" she said.

"She would dismiss you instantly," said Mr Chubb gravely. "She might," he added, "dismiss me too."

Fanny laughed.

"It is no laughing matter," said Mr Chubb, with what Fanny felt to be mock severity (though she hastily put on a serious expression). "No laughing matter at all. Cook is a very ferocious lady."

"So is ours," said Fanny with feeling, and stopped short in horror, realizing what she had said. "I mean," she went on hastily, "the last cook I met was ferocious."

"In Edinburgh?" said Mr Chubb.

Fanny nodded uncomfortably. She wished that she had never mentioned Edinburgh, that she had never started upon this ladder of lies. It was wicked to tell lies, of course, but she now saw that it could be inconvenient also. One thing leads to another, and before you know it there is no way of going back. She wished that she had told the Vicar the truth from the beginning, and then remembered that if she had done so he would undoubtedly have sent her straight back home. And with the thought of home, her problems raised their ugly heads again—the baby and what might or might not have happened to it and, now, the new problem that she had done yet another dreadful thing in running away.

"Dear me," said Mr Chubb. "Half-past six already. Nearly time for Evensong. Perhaps you would oblige me by making a cup of tea."

Only half-past six? The church clock had been striking six when Fanny left her own house. Have I really been a kitchen-maid for only half an hour, she thought despairingly. It had seemed more like days, weeks . . .

"Tea," said Mr Chubb again, and Fanny jumped. "Yes, please," she said, and then "Yes, sir," as she realized that had not been what he meant at all.

What about my tea? she thought, as she laboured to fill the great black kettle with water and lift it on to the top of the range. A picture of the nursery at home, warm with firelight and full of the smell of muffins and toast, blotted out the Vicar's kitchen for an instant, like an image of Heaven. I am being punished, thought Fanny miserably, for being so wicked. For asking for cherry tart and clotted cream and for not loving the new baby.

She made the tea—not without some difficulty, for

she had never done such a thing before and only knew
what to do from years of observing Nurse and Sukie at
home. Then she loaded a tray and found her way back
along those long dark corridors to Mr Chubb's study.

He was busy writing at the desk, and looked critically
at the tray over an untidy pile of papers. "Very nice.
Thank you. We shall have to consider making you a
parlour-maid."

Fanny's head was still full of her own wickedness. "No, thank you," she said, her mouth quivering as tears threatened once more. "I shall have to go on being a kitchen-maid for a long time because I am so wicked."

"Is that so?" said the Vicar. He poured himself a cup of tea and went on, "You are obliged to be a kitchen-maid because of your wickedness?"

"Yes," said Fanny.

"And do you suppose that all kitchen-maids are wicked?"

There was a short silence. "No," said Fanny, now thoroughly muddled.

"Hmmn," said the Vicar. He took a gulp of tea, put the cup down, looked intently at Fanny and said, "Supposing you sit down and tell me all about this wickedness."

Fanny hesitated. She did not want to tell anyone, and yet knew at the same time that it would be a great relief to do so. And who better than a Vicar? Vicars, after all, must be experts on wickedness.

She sat down, and told.

When she had finished there was a pause. Mr Chubb took off his glasses and polished them on his sleeve (which served only to make them a great deal dirtier). Then he put them back on again and said severely, "What nonsense!"

"Nonsense?" said Fanny. Nonsense was disapproved of too, at home, but it was a great deal better than wickedness.

"What nonsense," said the Vicar, "to suppose that

the Almighty, having gone to all that trouble to provide a new member of your family should decide to take her back again merely to oblige you."

"Oh," said Fanny, thoroughly abashed. Put like that the Vicar was entirely right. "But the cherry tart?" she went on anxiously "He sent the cherry tart."

"Cherry tart is another matter altogether," said the Vicar. "A mere trifle. I beg your pardon, I mean a mere cherry tart." And his large person heaved and shook and brought forth what was undoubtedly a laugh.

Fanny felt a twinge of indignation. She did not think that her affairs were anything to laugh about. She decided to abandon everything.

"And I have never been a kitchen-maid," she said. "And I haven't ever been to Edinburgh. So I have told lies as well."

"My dear," said the Vicar, "I never supposed otherwise. Kitchen-maids do not wear fur-trimmed Sunday coats."

"Oh," said Fanny, crestfallen.

"The same Sunday coat, indeed," said the Vicar, "that I observed in church this morning."

Fanny felt foolish, extremely foolish, but at the same time relieved of a great weight. It was the same feeling, vastly magnified, as the discovery that the cup you have just dropped is not, in fact, broken. If the Vicar did not consider her wicked then she could not, in fact, be wicked.

"You don't think then," she said, in a small voice, "that God will take the new baby back?"

"I very much doubt if He ever considered the matter," said Mr Chubb.

There was a silence. Fanny heaved a great sigh. If the Vicar said that, then that must be the case.

Mr Chubb finished his tea, put the cup down, and stood up. "And now," he said, "unless you wish to continue your career as a kitchen-maid . . ."

Fanny shook her head violently.

". . . I think I had better take you home. There is just time before Evensong, if I am not mistaken."

They walked together through the darkened streets, slowly because the Vicar's bad leg would not allow him to go very fast. And the slowness of the walk gave them time for what Fanny considered to be a very

interesting conversation during which the Vicar told her that he had been the youngest of a family of eleven children. "It is much worse to be the eldest," said Fanny with conviction, and the Vicar disputed this most persuasively with accounts of the fearful things done to him by his elder brothers and sisters till Fanny was hard put to it to maintain her side of the argument. They reached the door of Fanny's house just at the point when the Vicar had finished telling the story of a famous family fight between himself and one of his brothers, so that for a moment, in Fanny's mind, he was translated from an old man in a surplice, about to take Evensong, into an angry small boy in knickerbockers.

"Well," said the Vicar, "goodnight." And he held out his hand.

"Goodnight," said Fanny. And then, with a small flood of doubt, "You are certain . . . quite, quite certain . . . that the baby will be there?"

"Listen," said Mr Chubb.

And from the lighted nursery window at the top of the house, Fanny heard the noise of her newest sister wailing.

She went into the house, to be scolded for being late for tea, ("And where did you get to, miss, I'd like to know—up and down the stairs Sukie's been, looking for you high and low . . .") and to find that the muffins had been eaten by Albert. Which, such was Fanny's relief to be at home, did not send her into anything like the rage it would have done in the normal course of events.

And that, by and large, is the end of the story. What had happened, though, did have a profound effect upon Fanny's feelings both towards cherry tart and towards the new baby. She found that she could never bear to look at a cherry again, and the new baby (who was named Ethel) became her favourite among the Young Children—indeed her favourite sister. And on Sundays, after church, she and the Vicar would exchange the brief, private smiles of two people who know something that they have no intention of sharing with anyone else.

Fanny and the Monsters

For her tenth birthday, in 1866, Fanny received as
presents a doll, a needle-case and embroidery frame, a
story-book and a seed-pearl necklace. She had been
hoping for a microscope, a geological hammer, a
book about fossils and a butterfly net. She did her
best to smile nicely, and looked with particular
hatred at the doll, which was from her godmother,
Aunt Caroline.

It had a pudgy, pale wax face and a petulant
expression—indeed it looked a bit like Aunt Caroline,
which Fanny thought an especially disagreeable way
of looking. Aunt Caroline had come to tea, in order
to hand over her present. She sat on the drawing-room
sofa, stout and critical and rather deaf, and asked
Fanny a great many questions about how well she
could sew and whether she knew her catechism and if
she was setting a good example to her brothers and
sisters. Fanny was the eldest of eight, which she
considered a very unfair thing to have to be.

Mamma sat at the other end of the sofa, and from
time to time Aunt Caroline stopped asking Fanny

49

questions and made remarks about her to Mamma, as though she were a chair or a table or a dog. Fanny tried to endure this as best she could and prayed fervently for an early escape. She could hear Albert (her eldest brother and deadly rival) in the garden making clattering noises which involved, she strongly suspected, having borrowed her hoop without asking. She fidgeted and Aunt Caroline said, "Sit up straight, dear, little girls should sit still and keep quiet in the drawing-room." Then she said, "When you are a grown-up lady with children of your own you will know what I mean."

She looked at Fanny over the top of her spectacles and Fanny looked back at her sulkily and said, "I'm not going to be a grown-up lady. I'm going to be a palaeontologist."

Aunt Caroline took from her purse a small black ear-trumpet. She placed the ear-trumpet to her ear and said, "I beg your pardon?"

Fanny said very loudly, "I'm going to be a palaeontologist."

Aunt Caroline put the ear-trumpet down on her lap and said sternly, "I don't think that is at all a nice way for a little girl to talk." There was an odd tone to her voice—a faint note of doubt—and Fanny realized with satisfaction that Aunt Caroline didn't know what palaeontologist meant, but that nothing in the world was going to make her admit it.

So Fanny said, again very loudly, "A palaeontologist is a person who knows about rocks and fossils and things." At which Aunt Caroline glared and said that there was no need to shout, and little girls did not

teach their grandmothers to suck eggs, either. In fact, for a moment a full scale battle threatened between them until Mamma broke in hastily to offer Aunt Caroline another cup of tea and to tell Fanny that she might go away now back up to the schoolroom.

Fanny did not go back to the schoolroom, but into the garden to find Albert and settle the matter of the hoop. When she had done that (rather noisily but without actual bloodshed) she went down to the pond to make sure that no one had been interfering with her water-beetle collection and her tadpoles. Fanny was studying the habits of insects, birds and indeed anything else that would let her get close enough to study its habits. She was training herself to be a scientist. Her governess, Miss Purser, taught French and music and arithmetic and scripture and needle-work and writing and reading. She certainly did not teach science and had got very cross when Fanny suggested it. Miss Purser was also the governess of Albert and the other Old Children; the Young Children were still cosily in the nursery, having a nice time and not having to bother about anything they didn't want to.

Fanny squatted by the pond and watched a caddis fly. The caddis fly's proper Latin name was *Limnophilus*. Fanny liked knowing this kind of thing. She liked long and difficult words like inconsequential and Deuteronomy and acrimonious (she did not always know what they meant). She also enjoyed talking about flowers and insects rather grandly by their Latin names—partly because it was fun and partly to annoy Albert who did not know (or care) that a dandelion is *Taraxicum officinale* and a daisy *Bellis perennis*.

When at last Fanny went back into the house she found that she was in trouble. Firstly because she had left her doll in the middle of the lawn ("As though," said Mamma reprovingly, "you didn't like kind Aunt Caroline's present."); and secondly because her fight with Albert had been heard and observed from the drawing-room. Aunt Caroline had wondered if Fanny was perhaps becoming a rather boisterous little girl. Apparently it didn't matter if Albert was boisterous, a point which Fanny took note of as yet another instance of the unfairness of being not only the eldest but a girl at that. Albert, as a boy, was not only allowed (within limits) to be boisterous but was encouraged to do interesting things like go fishing and fly kites which were considered less suitable for girls.

Mamma finished her lecture and then went on, "But Aunt Caroline has very kindly offered to take you out for the day next week, as a birthday treat."

Fanny perked up a little at this. Admittedly, a day with Aunt Caroline had a limited appeal; it depended where they were going. She said, hopefully but without much confidence, "May we go to a waxwork exhibition?"

Mamma did not think that Aunt Caroline would care for waxworks.

"Or a fair?" said Fanny, with even less confidence.

"Certainly not," said Mamma. "Aunt Caroline is going to take you to the Crystal Palace. There! Now is that not a wonderful treat!"

Fanny received this news with mixed feelings. The Crystal Palace was known for its magnificent gardens and its display of works of art and sounded more like a treat for Aunt Caroline than for her. All the same, a trip to London in a train was no small matter, and the Crystal Palace was very famous and very amazing, and if Albert was not coming she would be able to annoy him afterwards with tales about it all. So she cheered up considerably and began to look forward to next week.

She set off in high spirits, despite having been obliged to wear her best dress and boots, which were stuffy and uncomfortable, and a hat with ribbons which she detested. Aunt Caroline was also got up for the occasion, in an immensely skirted dress of black bombasine from which her stout top and round face rose rather like a knob on top of a mushroom. She had a small hamper containing, Fanny observed with satisfaction, some cold chicken, various pies and cakes and a bottle of fruit cordial. She also had a bottle of sal volatile in case they should feel faint, handkerchiefs doused in eau de cologne and lavender water in case they should come across bad smells, an umbrella, and a small folding stool in case there should be nowhere to sit down. Thus equipped, she settled herself into the corner of the railway carriage and spent the journey complaining about draughts and smuts.

Fanny sat beside her and read the story-book that Aunt Caroline had given her for her birthday. The book was about two girls. One of them was a disobedient, rude and noisy girl called Jemima who refused to mend her ways and therefore fell ill of consumption and eventually died, a process which was described in much detail over many pages. The other girl, Emma, was kind to animals and poor people and a joy and comfort to her parents, as a result of which she had a rather unlikely meeting with a very rich man who died the next day and left her all his money. Fanny considered this a remarkably silly story, and in any case unfair on the rich man—*he* hadn't done anything wrong. That sort of thing, as anyone can see, doesn't happen in real life where some people who are perfectly horrid (such as Miss Purser, her governess) are very well and busy living happily ever afterwards, while others who are nicer in every way have a very nasty time indeed. So she read the book resentfully (what she had really wanted was a grown-up book about fossils or shells or butterflies with a great many diagrams and illustrations and difficult Latin names) and then looked out of the window, where the country was giving way to black, smoky, busy London.

The journey got more and more interesting. There were crowds of people to look at and all sorts of vulgar and distasteful sights to excite Aunt Caroline, such as acrobats performing on the pavement outside the station and women wearing outlandish hats that Aunt Caroline suspected might even be French. They changed onto another train which took them right to the entrance to the Crystal Palace gardens, and there was the Crystal Palace itself, glittering in the sunshine for all the world like an enormous greenhouse, with a long wide avenue leading to it and fountains and terraces and flights of steps and great throngs of people. They set off along this avenue, and then all of a sudden Fanny's attention was caught by a notice pointing down another path which led away beyond some trees towards a lake.

The notice said TO THE PREHISTORIC MONSTERS.

Fanny gasped. She seized Aunt Caroline's hand, and pointed to the notice. "Please," she said. "Can't we go and see them?"

Aunt Caroline peered at the notice and then said

firmly, "No dear. That is the kind of thing that gives children nightmares. You don't want to have nightmares, do you?"

Fanny opened her mouth to say she was perfectly prepared to take the risk, but Aunt Caroline was already off again in full sail in the direction of the Crystal Palace, her skirts bouncing and billowing in the breeze and the hamper clutched in one hand. Fanny cast one more longing look in the direction of the prehistoric monsters and followed her, a little sullenly.

Inside, the Palace was rather like an enormous light and airy railway station into which a garden had been brought. There were palms and ferns everywhere, through which peered huge statues of sphinxes. The sphinxes were part of a great display of all the different kinds of art in the world. There were statues on all sides, standing about amid the greenery, many of them with no clothes on at all, which Aunt Caroline found upsetting. She hurried past these with her eyes down. Fanny found them boring rather than upsetting. She trailed along behind Aunt Caroline and began to feel cross and tired. Aunt Caroline looked round and said that on no account must they get separated. In such a vast and crowded place they could easily lose one another altogether. Fanny caught up with her, and stood patiently while Aunt Caroline studied a display of Greek vases. Fanny yawned. Aunt Caroline moved on to an immense plaster frieze of people fighting each other.

What Fanny did next was so wicked that I really do not know that I should be telling you about it.

She took one quick look backwards to make sure that Aunt Caroline was not watching her from behind a cast-iron pillar or an eruption of potted ferns, and then shot off through the crowds as fast as she could go, out of the Crystal Palace and down the avenue towards the lake and that enticing notice.

She followed the path between bushes and flowerbeds, very uncertain as to what she was going to find. Would the prehistoric monsters be stuffed, or would they be in cages like animals at a zoo? Or what? There were not so many people around here and none

of the ones coming from the direction of the lake looked pale or shaken, so Fanny decided that whatever there was to see could not be so very alarming. She licked her lips at the thought of recounting all this to Albert, and then remembered with irritation that she would not be able to, or Albert would undoubtedly tell on her and everyone would know she had got lost on purpose.

The lake, which was quite large, was on one side of her, and on the other was a path which wound off at one end of it, up and down through little woodland glades. She came round a corner, and found herself looking across a small stretch of water at an island. The island was covered with trees and bushes, and there among the trees and bushes . . .

. . . There among the trees and bushes—oh marvel of marvels!—was the most enormous, terrifying, utterly unexpected creature, rearing up on its hind-legs, rust red in colour, and apparently chewing the

leaves off a chestnut tree. For a moment Fanny was about to turn tail and flee, until she saw that the monster was a statue—albeit a most life-like and convincing statue, but a statue nonetheless.

And now, looking round, she saw that there were monsters all over the lake island. Some of them peered from the undergrowth, only their great scaly heads and gnashing teeth visible, while other crocodile-like creatures lounged half in the water where little parties of ducks—real ducks—cruised among them and even sat on them, preening. Green and red and shiny brown, the monsters strode about their island jungle, their mouths opened to shriek and bellow into the smoky London skies, their great claws plunged into the London mud and their tails lashing the still waters of the lake. One great creature—tyrannosaurus rex—towered above a birch tree, silhouetted against the skyline; you only had to close your eyes to imagine its awful trumpetings and the clash of its dreadful teeth. Fanny, gazing, shivered deliciously.

And the names, the names were wonderful beyond belief: megalosaurus and plesiosaurus and iguanodon and teleosaurus and ichthyosaurus. She wandered to and fro, reading the names and admiring the monsters and so absorbed in it all that she did not look where she was going at all and walked smack into a person who was standing at the side of the path looking at a particularly extravagant monster called labyrinthodont.

Fanny apologized. The person—who was a young-ish gentleman, rather untidily dressed and with a lot of black beard—said absent-mindedly, "Don't mention it." And then he added, possibly to himself, "The rear limbs are inaccurate, of course." He was still looking at the labyrinthodont.

Fanny said, "I beg your pardon?"

The young man seemed hardly to notice that she was a little girl. He began to talk to her as though she were somebody quite grown-up and significant. The model of the labyrinthodont, he explained, was

wrong in that in his opinion the back legs should be considerably larger and thicker, and also the neck should, he thought, be higher. When Fanny asked how he could possibly know this, he explained that it is possible to get a very good idea of what creatures like this—which should properly be called dinosaurs— looked like from their fossil bones which are found in rocks. But there are different opinions, and the young man considered that the sculptor of the dinosaurs—while doing an admirable job in general— was wrong in a few details. The young man added that he was studying fossil creatures and hoped one day to write a book about them; Fanny realized with awe that she was in the presence of a real palae-ontologist.

She gazed at the young man in admiration and hung on his every word. Somehow the fact that he was quite young made him even more impressive—she had imagined all scientists as being very ancient and white-haired. She asked him a great many questions, which he did not seem to mind at all. He told her that dinosaurs had all become extinct many millions of years ago, and that when they were swimming and striding around England there were no mammals or birds such as we know at all. And that before the dinosaurs there had been other strange creatures, reptiles and fish-like things and shells and worms. Fanny, remembering the illustration at the beginning of her Bible, in which Adam and Eve, looking rather self-conscious and wearing what appeared to be bath-towels, were standing underneath a tree eating apples and surrounded by sheep and cows and deer and lions and tigers, said, "Then there must have been dinosaurs in the Garden of Eden?"

The young man looked thoughtful. He stroked his beard and said that one had to suppose that there must have been. "Since God created everything all at once," said Fanny, "I expect He made them on the fifth day, along with the fowls of the air and the creeping things."

At this the young man stroked his beard even more, and looked worried. And then he began to talk most interestingly about a famous scientist called Charles Darwin, whom the young man admired very much. This Mr Darwin believed that living creatures—birds and animals and plants—had not all come into being at one and the same time, but were in a constant state of change and development. Some creatures, like the dinosaurs, had died out altogether and become extinct, while others had adapted themselves, grown different teeth or fur or wings, or altered their shape to become something quite different. "Like," said the young man, waving his arms about in excitement, "like you and me and our ancestors, the apes and monkeys."

Fanny's eyes grew rounder and rounder. According to this Mr Darwin, people—her and Aunt Caroline and the young man and even the Queen herself—were all descended from monkeys. Monkeys were a kind of poor relation, as it were, who had not succeeded in developing large brains and getting cleverer and cleverer.

All families of creatures, the young man explained— so loudly and enthusiastically that several passers-by turned to stare—are divided into different kinds, species, and when a species is no good at adapting itself to the kind of world it has to live in, it dies out, like the dinosaurs.

"Too ugly?" said Fanny helpfully.

Not so much too ugly, the young man thought, as too big and cumbersome. Or perhaps the climate changed and they were unable to change with it.

Fanny considered all this, and the more she considered the more sensible it all seemed. Furthermore, she liked monkeys, and found the idea of being distantly related to them rather attractive.

Then, because she by now thought the young man quite the nicest and most entertaining person she had ever met, she confided to him how she was, in fact, in a small way, a scientist herself. She told him about her beetle collection and the tadpoles and her lists of wildflowers and (by the way, as it were) about the disastrous birthday presents and Albert and how much she hated French and arithmetic and needlework and a great many other things besides. And the young man listened gravely and nodded from time to time. He said it must indeed be very trying, and one could only recommend that she continue with her studies on her own. He said that if at any point he could be of any assistance he would be only too delighted. He fished in his waistcoat pocket and produced his card, which he handed to Fanny with a little bow, quite as though she were a grown-up lady. The card said 'Dr J. P. Halliday, M.A., F.R.S., Department of Palae-ontology, British Museum, London'.

Fanny positively glowed. She went bright pink with

pleasure and embarrassment. She tucked the card into her pocket and was trying to think of the right thing to say when the young man took his watch out, exclaimed that it was far later than he had thought, raised his hat once more, said that it had been a pleasure to make her acquaintance, and departed.

Fanny made a final inspection of the monsters—she had quite learned them by heart now—and set off back to the Crystal Palace, wondering rather nervously how she was going to find Aunt Caroline and what Aunt Caroline would have to say when she did find her. In fact she became more and more anxious and upset, and more and more sorry that she had done what she had, so that tears began to trickle down her cheeks as she hunted about in the crowds for Aunt Caroline. At last she found a policeman towering over her saying kindly, "Now then, missy, what's up with you, then? Lost your Mamma, have you?" Fanny nodded tearfully and the policeman led her off to a room at the back of the Palace. And there was Aunt Caroline, also distraught, mopping herself with her eau de cologne handkerchief and occasionally sniffing at her sal volatile bottle. And she was so relieved to see Fanny again—and indeed Fanny was so relieved to see her—that they were reunited without any mention being made of how Fanny had been so silly as to get herself lost.

Indeed, they had a very pleasant journey home, keeping their strength up from time to time with goodies from Aunt Caroline's hamper. Fanny watched Aunt Caroline's struggles to get her skirts through the train door and then to sit down between two equally billowing ladies (thus clamping a small man at the end so tightly that he looked in grave danger of being snuffed out altogether) and wondered if she, like the dinosaurs, was heading for extinction. Certainly she looked equally ill-adapted to the world.

At home, Fanny nursed her secret. It was frustrating, to say the least of it, not to be able to mention to Albert, casually, that she was personally acquainted with a member of the British Museum. Or that she had seen creatures such as would make your hair stand on end, beside which the dragons and ogres of fairy stories were as nothing. That she knew a brontosaurus from a pterodactyl and an iguanadon from a plesiosaurus. Sometimes, she could hardly restrain herself and indeed on one occasion came very close to disaster.

It was at Sunday dinner-time. Fanny and Albert, as the eldest, were allowed to have Sunday dinner in the dining-room with Mamma and Papa instead of in the nursery with the other children, where they had the rest of their meals. Fanny enjoyed this, because the food was very much better and it made her feel important and grown-up, even if it did mean being on your best behaviour. She liked grown-up conversations; conversations in the nursery were not at all grown-up as you can imagine with seven other children aged eight, seven, five, four, three, two and one, and Nurse who spent most of her time telling people to eat up their rice pudding and take their elbows off the table and not talk with their mouths full. Jane, Susan and Ethel, the three youngest, had no conversation at all to speak of, while that of Charles, Harriet, Emma and Albert was mostly argument and demands for more.

So Fanny always enjoyed Sunday dinner, where people listened to what you said and did not interrupt each other and you could talk about more interesting things.

It was through this, though, that the trouble arose. Papa was talking of the Vicar's sermon in church that morning, and complaining that the Vicar had taken to speaking indistinctly so that he had not heard it all properly. Now Fanny had been less concerned with not hearing properly than with what the Vicar had been saying, which was all about the Creation and the Garden of Eden and which had put her in mind of her friend Mr Halliday and everything that he had said to her. So when Papa had finished she broke in, enthusiastically but rashly, about a famous man that she had heard of called Mr Darwin who believed that . . . And as she spoke Papa's eyebrows gathered in a great stormy black line, a danger-sign which Fanny would have recognized if she had not been so busy with what she was saying.

". . . so Mr Darwin says we are all descended from monkeys," she concluded, "is that not interesting? And he thinks that . . ."

Papa put his knife and fork down with a clatter. "I will not have that man's name spoken in my house," he thundered. Albert gazed in amazement, and Mamma dabbed her mouth nervously with her napkin.

"But Papa . . ." Fanny began.

Papa rose to his feet. Everybody stopped eating and watched him with apprehension. "Blasphemous rubbish!" roared Papa, "Never let me hear such talk in my home again." And he sat down with a thump and attacked his roast beef with such ferocity that one might have thought it was the dinner that had given voice to such outrageous ideas and not his daughter. Fanny, glad to be out of the line of fire, sat tight and said no more.

Now it should be explained that Papa was by no means unusual in reacting thus to the notion that the Victorian English gentleman, such as himself, had evolved very slowly over millions of years from an ape instead of tracing his ancestry to Adam in the Garden of Eden. As far as he was concerned, these views were very shocking indeed, and he was not prepared to consider them any further. Indeed, he was so busy being indignant that he quite forgot to ask Fanny wherever she had heard such things, for which she was much relieved.

Fanny, remembering what her friend from the Crystal Palace gardens had said, continued with her scientific researches on her own. This was not always easy. People were very unsympathetic and uncooperative. The cook, for some reason, objected very much when she discovered that Fanny was keeping a bowl of frog-spawn in the larder to see whether or not it would hatch out indoors. The gardener took exception to her experiment to see if roses, when watered with ammonia, will produce a nasty smell. And Nurse behaved in a completely unreasonable way

when Fanny's spider collection escaped in the nursery. As for what Miss Purser said when Fanny brought a dead mouse to lessons because she thought it would be interesting to dissect it, I think we had better not go into that.

It wasn't at all easy to work under such conditions. Fanny did the best she could, however, and was quietly satisfied when two of her tadpoles successfully became frogs. And then, one day when she and Albert and Emma and Harriet were being taken for a walk by Miss Purser, a very significant thing happened.

Fanny's home was in the country on the outskirts of a large village. The village consisted mainly of small stone cottages, in front of whose windows Fanny passed, trailing irritably behind the others. She had had an argument with Albert which had not been satisfactorily concluded because Miss Purser had decided that they must stick to the lanes and not go in the fields (where Fanny would have been able to search for insects and wild flowers). There might be mud in the fields, said Miss Purser, or damp or cows or nettles; Miss Purser became quite hysterical when faced with horrors such as these. Fanny stumped along, and from time to time she glanced into the cottage windows, which were like little dark murky tanks, with sometimes a potted plant on the windowsill, or a cat curled up like a bun and squinting out into the street.

And then all of a sudden there on one of the windowsills was something entirely different.

It was a fossil. A very large honey-coloured fossil like a catherine wheel. An ammonite, as Fanny well knew.

She stared in fascination. After a moment or two a face came to the window and stared back at her: an old man's face. Fanny looked away in confusion, and then, because she couldn't help it, back at that irresistible fossil. The cottage door opened and the old man said, "Eh?"

Miss Purser and the others were now at the far end of the village street. The old man continued, "You wantin' something, missy?"

"No, thank you," said Fanny hastily, backing away. And then, because the old man didn't after all look particularly fierce or unfriendly, she added, "Please . . . I wondered . . . I was just looking at the fossil in your window. Where did you find it?"

The old man, it appeared, was a retired quarryman. He had spent all his life working in the quarry nearby—which Fanny knew, although only by repute because it was a place most strictly out of bounds to all the children, as being unsafe, dirty and frequented by undesirable people. The quarryman, though, didn't seem to be at all undesirable. He told Fanny that he and his friends often found fossils in the rock, and sometimes after they had been blasting whole bones and teeth could be seen. "Monsters, see," said the old man, "monsters such as there was in these parts in olden days." Fanny felt a great surge of excitement. This was turning out not to have been such a disagreeable walk after all. She asked the quarryman

some more questions until Emma came rushing back down the street to say that Miss Purser was in a very bad mood and Fanny was to come along at once.

All the way home Fanny thought.

She thought about how wrong it is to do what you have been told not to do. She thought how annoying it would be if she had an accident in the quarry and everyone (especially Albert) was able to say, "I told you so". Except that perhaps in that case she would be dead, which would be even worse than being annoyed. But most of all she thought about dinosaurs.

And at last she decided that if she were very careful and sensible . . . if she did not climb or scramble, and spoke to no one—whether desirable or undesirable— no great harm could come of it . . .

She picked an afternoon when Miss Purser was suffering from a bad headache and consequently paying less attention than usual to what the children were doing. She slipped out of the garden by the back gate, through the village, along the lane and over the fields in the direction of the quarry.

Everything was quiet, but as she got nearer to the quarry the grass and hedges began to be covered with a powdery white dust. She could hear a distant tap-tap of picks, and, once or twice, men shouting to one another. She went through a gate and out onto a track quite bleached and white with dust, and there beyond was the quarry, like a great pale stony gash in the landscape.

Fanny had arrived, quite by accident, at the best

place for seeing what was going on. She was standing at the edge of a part of the quarry that must have been disused for some time, because grass and weeds were growing up again among the tumbled stones. Here, the sides were not steep or dangerous, but at the far end, where she could see several men at work, distant whitish figures chipping away at the rock-face, there were high shelving cliffs, crowned with a skin of turf and waving flowers, just like the cliffs at the sea-side. Fanny resolved to keep away from there.

Then, all of a sudden, there was a burst of activity from the quarry-workers. One of them, who had been climbing up the rock-face, came scrambling down. He waved and shouted something at his companions, who all abandoned what they were at and trotted away from the cliff and round a corner into another part of the quarry, where they retreated behind some large boulders and sat down in a row. Fanny watched in bewilderment.

And then she realized the significance of all this. There was a shattering boom, that made her ears ring and shook the very ground under her feet. The whole world seemed to quiver, and then a great balloon of white dust sprang from the cliff, and there was a long, shivery thunderous roar.

Of course . . . blasting. Blasting the rock away.

Fanny felt herself all over gingerly to make sure she had not been blasted too, but she seemed to be much as she had been before, if a little dusty, and indeed the quarrymen were now ambling slowly back to the bottom of the cliff. Fanny, too curious to go on being so very cautious and restrained, advanced a little way into the quarry in order to get a better view.

Gradually, the dust cleared, showing where the blast had made a kind of avalanche down the far side of the quarry. The quarrymen were busy clearing away the loose stone. Presently, though, someone blew a whistle and they all gathered up their tools and began to move off across the floor of the quarry, towards where Fanny was standing. She ducked down behind the hedge and watched them go past, quite near, talking about how they would blast again in a few days' time. "Finish off that face, see," said one of them, who appeared to be in charge. "That weren't a big enough one, all that face got to come down."

Fanny waited until they had gone, and then advanced gingerly further into the quarry. She felt very nervous, hoping that the men had not left stray bits of gunpowder around and that she had not got the hem of her dress betrayingly dusty and that there were none of these undesirable people about.

On the contrary, it was so very quiet and still that after a while she began to feel she would have preferred company. There was nothing at all to be heard except birds and the occasional rustling of the wind in a bush or tree. And the rustling and the silence combined made her feel extremely uneasy and just a little as though she were *not* alone . . .

Suppose everyone had made an unfortunate mistake and dinosaurs had *not* become extinct after all and here in this very place . . .

Something like a heavy footfall to one side made her swing round with a little gasp. There was nothing there; just a spot on the cliff-face where the dust was rising again. A rock must have fallen. Fanny resolved to keep well away. She took a quick look all round. There was nothing and no one.

Scientists, she told herself sternly, are not afraid of things that aren't possible. Such as dinosaurs in Oxfordshire in 1865. In fact, scientists aren't afraid of anything, they are very sensible, matter-of-fact people who . . .

She gave a jump and a little shriek.

A pheasant. Bursting out of the undergrowth with that stupid pheasant clatter and yell. Not a pterodactyl or an iguanadon. An ordinary everyday pheasant.

Control yourself, said Fanny to Fanny sternly.

About fifteen or twenty yards away from the place where the men had set off the blast she stopped, well out of the way of any more falling rocks. The explosion had sent stones flying all over the place, so that there was a great deal of loose stuff lying around where she stood, and after a few minutes, to her joy and excitement, she spotted a chunk with a cluster of small shell-like fossils embedded in it. She picked it up, and began to search for more. But her luck had run out and she found nothing.

It must be getting late. High time to go home before her absence was discovered. She took one last look around her, and then up at the cliff-face. It was easy to pick out the part that had been newly exposed today by the blast because it was like a pale, raw scar, with a great beard of loose rocks and dust flowing from it. It made a shape like a longish bearded face, with a crown of green hair—grass and bushes—at the top. And in the middle of it there was another shape, a funny shape, a kind of long knobbly shape almost like a tail, with a bent leg coming from it, and the other end disappearing into the part of the rock that had not yet been blasted. The more you looked at it the more you could imagine . . .

. . . A monster. An iguanadon. Or a brontosaurus, as it might be. Or a plethiosaurus or an ichthyosaurus.

Fanny blinked. She shut her eyes tight and then

opened them again. She took a few steps forward and stared a bit more.

If . . . if by a wonderful and amazing chance that *was* what she was looking at, then why was the tail so knobbly? Why not smooth like the tails of the Crystal Palace monsters? Fanny hugged herself as she stared and stared at the rock, and as she did so her fingers met her ribs at either side and everything fell neatly into place. Of course! Fossils are bones—stone bones. And what she was looking at was the bony outline of the whatever-it-might-be up there on the side of the quarry, hidden for millions upon millions of years and now suddenly revealed by a blast of gunpowder.

Unless, of course, she was imagining the whole thing. Like clouds if looked at long enough become castles or whales or cathedrals or trumpet-blowing angels.

But the more she stared the more certain she became.

It was really very late now. Reluctantly, she turned and began to hurry home. What was to be done? That was the problem. For, remembering the snatch of conversation overheard as the quarrymen passed her, that bit of rock would undoubtedly be blasted again within a few days, and the dinosaur blown to smithereens.

As soon as Fanny got home (mercifully Miss Purser was still much taken up with her headache and had not even noticed her absence) she rushed to the cupboard in which her best dress was kept and searched its pockets. Triumph! The card was still there. She took a page from her copy-book, went into a corner of the schoolroom, and began furtively to write.

After a long time and much chewing of the end of the pen, she had written a reasonably neat and tidy letter. 'Dear Sir,' it ran, 'Please come quickly there is no time to be lost or it will be blown up for ever. It is in the quarry by our village, Shipton village, in Oxfordshire. I think it is an iguanadon. I found it nobody else knows about it. Please come. Yours respectfully, Fanny Stanton (Miss).' As an afterthought she added a postscript: 'Only the tail and one leg are to be seen but I am sure.' Then, seized with sudden doubt, 'I am the young lady you spoke to in the Crystal Palace gardens.' She put the letter in an envelope, addressed it with great care to Dr J. P. Halliday at the British Museum in London, bought a stamp at the village post office and posted it.

Since Fanny's daily life was full of distractions—both agreeable and disagreeable—such as lessons and meals and warfare with Albert and attending to her various scientific experiments, she only thought off and on of the quarry and the dinosaur and her letter over the next few days. Indeed, for long periods she forgot the whole matter.

It was at such a point, when Fanny was in the schoolroom wrestling with some particularly difficult (and, in Fanny's opinion, entirely unnecessary) French verbs, that Mary the parlourmaid arrived to announce, in tones of some surprise, that Miss Fanny was wanted downstairs. There was a gentleman, Mary said, who had called and asked for her, and was even now with her Mamma and Papa in the drawing-room.

Fanny went down, at first mystified and with an automatic feeling of guilt (one was usually only summoned to the drawing-room because one was in disgrace) and then with rising interest. Could it possibly be . . . ?

And indeed it was. There was Dr Halliday, looking

much as he had looked in the Crystal Palace gardens—
that is to say, a trifle unkempt and dishevelled and
very bearded—and there were Mamma and Papa, both
looking perplexed, to say the least of it. Papa wore a
somewhat ominous frown. He said, "Fanny, this
gentleman tells us that you and he are acquainted."

Fanny nodded.

"And it appears that you have written him a
letter?"

"Just a very small letter," murmured Fanny. It was
apparent from Papa's tone that writing letters to
strange gentlemen was not the proper thing to do.
She was beginning to feel extremely nervous now, as
it occurred to her that a whole chain of wickednesses
were about to be—perhaps already had been—
revealed, from visiting the Crystal Palace monsters
to going to the quarry.

However, it was also apparent that Dr Halliday's
card, which Papa was holding, had a certain persuasive
power. "British Museum . . ." grunted Papa. And
now Dr Halliday began to talk to Mamma and Papa
about his work, with the same enthusiasm that he had
to Fanny. He talked of fossils and dinosaurs and
Mamma said gracious! the very idea of such terrible
creatures made her feel quite faint, and Papa began to
look distinctly impressed, and Fanny hoped fervently
that Dr Halliday would not be so unwise as to
mention Mr Darwin or monkeys.

And the upshot of it all was that after a while
Fanny and Papa and Dr Halliday went off together to

the quarry. "I sincerely hope," said Papa sternly, "I most sincerely hope, Fanny, that you have not brought this gentleman down here on a wild goose chase," and Fanny realized that Papa had entirely shifted his point of view, so that now she would be in trouble if she could *not* produce a dinosaur.

The quarrymen were at work. Fanny led the way across the floor of the quarry. "I trust," Papa said with a scowl, "that my daughter is not wasting your time, Dr Halliday." To which Dr Halliday replied that he had the utmost confidence in Miss Stanton's powers of observation.

Fanny stopped, and turned to Dr Halliday, and pointed at the cliff face. "There," she said, and held her breath.

Papa peered. Dr Halliday stared, and then he turned to Fanny and shook her warmly by the hand. "Miss Stanton, I congratulate you," he said. Fanny turned bright pink.

"Iguanadon," said Dr Halliday. "You were quite correct. A remarkable specimen. Mr Stanton," he went on, to Papa, "you have an extremely perceptive daughter." Fanny went even pinker, if possible (she was not certain what perceptive meant, but it was clearly a good thing to be). Papa, who was still peering rather doubtfully at the rock, gave Fanny a startled look, as though he had never really seen her properly before, and said that every effort was made to ensure that his children took an intelligent interest in the wonders of nature. Fanny, remembering French

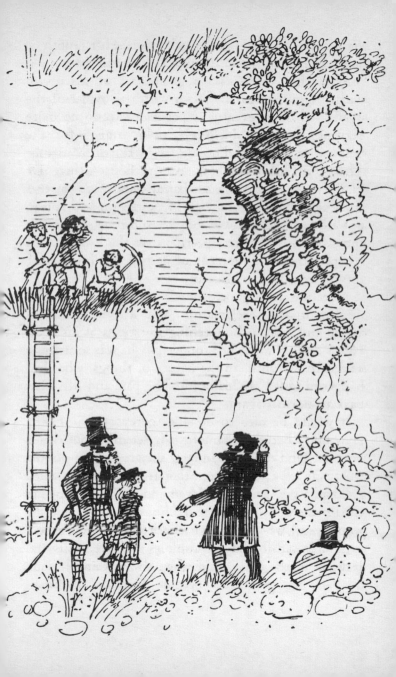

verbs and sums and needlework, opened her mouth to comment on this, and then thought better of it.

After that, there was a great deal of discussion with the quarrymen and then with the owner of the quarry, who was eventually persuaded to do no more blasting until Dr Halliday could arrange for the removal of the fossil dinosaur to the British Museum. Then they all went back to the house where Dr Halliday shook hands with Fanny once more (by this time news of these unheard-of goings-on had spread upwards to the nursery and schoolroom, so that all the other children were peering over the banisters, to complete Fanny's moment of glory), and invited her to visit him at the Museum.

After he had gone, there was a great deal of discussion and exclamation and a few questions asked, but not such searching questions as to spoil Fanny's day. Indeed, for some time she was something of a heroine, until, in the nature of things, what had happened faded gradually into the past and life went back to normal again.

It would be nice to be able to report that Fanny grew up to become a famous lady scientist, but this is not that kind of story. In fact, she grew up to do just what was expected of her—that is to say she married and had a good many children and spent most of her time being bothered about the housekeeping. But she was always, where her own children were concerned, extremely sensible about tadpoles and pet snails and seaweed in the bath. And when she was an old lady one of her grandsons became Curator of Small

Mammals at London Zoo, which pleased Fanny very much indeed.

As for the monsters, they are still in the Crystal Palace gardens, as large as life and almost as natural, and you can visit them any time you like.

Fanny and the Battle
of Potter's Piece

"I am a famous explorer," said Fanny, "and Albert is my faithful servant Bloggs, and Emma is my gun-bearer, and the rest are porters and pack-ponies." She started to wriggle through the hedge into Potter's Piece.

Albert objected that it was his turn to be leader, and the Young Children began to argue about which were porters and which were ponies. "Come on," said Fanny impatiently, "or you shan't play." And after a minute or two everybody swarmed after her. They crawled out into the long grass, where Fanny shot a lion or two, and peered cautiously down the slope to the stream and the tumble-down pigsty. Albert consulted the compass and declared them to be approaching the equator, Fanny pointed out the source of the Nile, and Charles had an encounter with a buffalo which involved everybody climbing a tree until it had been dealt with by Albert.

Fanny was the eldest of the Stantons. After her, in age order, came Albert and Emma (the Old Children) and Harriet and Charles and Jane and Susan and Ethel (the Young Children). Susan and Ethel, being only babies, stayed in the nursery and did not join in the Potter's Piece games—which Nurse and Papa and Mamma did not know about anyway. Potter's Piece was a stretch of waste ground that separated the Stanton's house from Next Door. Or rather, separated the two gardens. The Stantons' garden, which was very large, had a high wall round part of it and a high thick bristly hedge round the rest, both of which were meant to keep intruders out and the Stanton children in. The children were strictly forbidden to go outside into the road. But Potter's Piece was not the road, and long ago the children had discovered the existence of a convenient, child-sized tunnel through the hedge into it. They had decided, after some thought, that it might be more sensible not to mention this to the grown-ups just in case it occurred to anyone to block it up.

Whenever they felt like it they played in Potter's Piece. It was their place, their personal and private place. Perhaps it was because of this—the privacy and secrecy of the matter—that the Stantons hardly ever quarrelled when they were in Potter's Piece. They were like most families; a great deal of warfare was waged a great deal of the time. Girls against boys,

Old Children against Young Children, anybody against anybody. Fanny and Albert in particular had a noisy and quite enjoyable running argument about practically everything. But in Potter's Piece they stopped all this and got down to whatever it was they were playing. No one else knew about it because no one else went there. The gardener from Next Door occasionally looked through Next Door's side gate, but old Mr Sanders, who lived in the house all by himself except for his housekeeper and the maids, never showed his face.

"Ssh!" said Fanny. "Native drums!" The children flattened themselves under some bushes, and the Young Children shivered deliciously. Fanny's pretences were so real that they were never quite sure what was happening and what wasn't. Jane, who was not quite three, was firmly convinced that there were tigers in the shrubbery and Red Indians behind the greenhouses. Since she didn't know what either tigers or Red Indians were this just made life even more interesting and unexpected than it already was.

The children crouched down. "Load the blunderbuss!" whispered Fanny, and Emma began obediently to fiddle around with a forked branch and some hazel nuts.

Then suddenly they realized that the noises they were hearing were not imaginary at all. There really were voices coming from the spinney on the far side of the stream, beside Next Door's garden wall. There really was someone making a chopping sound and someone else crashing about in the dead leaves. They froze.

Out of the spinney came two boys of around Albert's age. Followed by a girl. Followed by three smaller children.

The Stantons sat up, trembling with indignation. How dare they! Who were they? Fanny and Albert stared, first at the strangers, and then at each other. Fanny was pink with outrage. Albert was spluttering. "They can't come here! They've got no business! Just wait till I . . ."

They broke cover. They stood up and went galloping down the hill towards the invaders, who watched them coming with casual interest. The two parties confronted each other across the stream.

Fanny said, "Where've you come from?"

Albert added, "This is our place. No one comes here but us."

"Go away!" chirped Jane, helpfully.

The invaders regarded them coolly. A boy with a lot of fair hair, wearing a sailor suit, said, "Who says?"

"Who says what?" retorted Fanny.

"Who says this is your place?"

"We do. It always has been."

"It's ours now," said the boy. He looked around. "Not bad. We're going to dam the stream and we may chop down some of those bushes for a house." He strolled away, slashing at nettles with a stick.

"You can't!" bellowed Albert, crimson with fury. "We'll stop you!"

"How?" said one of the girl invaders, looking interested.

Albert could think of no immediate reply to this. He huffed and puffed and stamped around like an angry bull.

The sailor-suited boy looked over his shoulder and said airily, "We might let you use that bit at the top over there, by the hedge."

The Stantons were reduced to speechlessness by this. They simply stood and gasped. Fanny was clenching her fists so hard that she later found a row of little dents where her nails had dug into her hands. Albert was practically steaming.

And then they heard from beyond their hedge the familiar sound of Sukie, the nursery maid, calling them in for dinner. A hasty retreat was necessary before Sukie discovered where they were. They were practised by now at melting through the hedge again so as to be found innocently playing in the garden. They gave the invaders one last ferocious glare. As they scrambled out into the garden they heard merry laughter from Potter's Piece.

Fanny, Albert and Emma were so upset by the whole affair that they could not eat their dinner, and the Young Children, who were given to imitation, did likewise. At which Nurse decided they must all be sickening for something, and made them each have a tablespoonful of what was known as the Dreadful Medicine. The Dreadful Medicine was dark brown and tasted of dead leaves, sea-water, tobacco and burnt rice pudding. It was used by Nurse for everything from stomach pains to toothache, and even on occasions as a punishment.

They were only just beginning to recover from it all later in the afternoon when Sukie came bouncing into the nursery to say that everybody was wanted by Mamma downstairs in the drawing-room, clean, wearing best clothes and the girls with their hair curled. There was a united howl of protest. Nurse sighed, picked up the curling tongs, and set to work.

"*Why?*" snarled Fanny, writhing as Sukie combed her hair. "Ouch! Ow! Why?"

"Because," said Sukie importantly, "the new lady from next door is coming over for tea, and you're to come down all of you and say how do you do nicely."

"What new lady?"

"Mrs Robinson that's bought the house from Mr Sanders. Mr Sanders is gone to live by the sea for his health. I'd have thought you'd have known that. Keep still now."

Since Mr Sanders was of no interest to the children, they had paid no attention to his departure. So there were new neighbours? Fanny considered this, and decided that that was of no interest either. She put on her best muslin dress, grumbling, and went over to Nurse, resignedly, to have her hair curled—a hideous process that involved winding hanks of hair up tightly in red hot tongs and holding them like that until the curl stayed put. It was like having your hair pulled out and being half fried both at once. By the time Fanny, Emma, Harriet and Jane were all curled everybody was wailing and Nurse was red in the face with irritation and exertion. Susan was let off, being so young, but even she had been stuffed into a clean dress, frilled and ribboned. Ethel was allowed to stay in the nursery in her cot. Albert and Charles were wearing their Sunday suits and their most uncomfortable boots.

They trooped down the stairs. The Stantons lived in a very large house with several floors. The different sections of the family were in layers: Nurse and the children in the nursery on the top floor, Miss Purser the governess and the Old Children in the schoolroom on the next floor during lesson-time in the mornings, Papa and Mamma in the drawing-room and the study and the library and the breakfast-room on the ground floor, and Cook and the maids in the kitchen and sculleries in the basement. Sometimes people got mixed up, but mostly they stayed in their own places. The Young Children, for instance, only came to the drawing-room on special occasions and never to the dining-room, though the Old Children ate Sunday lunch there with Mamma and Papa. It was one of the few advantages of being an Old Child. Mostly, being an Old Child meant disagreeable things like lessons with Miss Purser and church on Sundays and Setting a Good Example.

Fanny liked tea in the drawing-room when it was tea just with Mamma. Tea with visitors she liked rather less. That meant best behaviour and not more than one slice of cake and sitting up straight and not interrupting. The more Mamma wished the visitor to be given a good impression, the better the behaviour had to be and the more fuss was made about clean clothes and tormented hair. This Mrs Robinson was obviously meant to be given a very good impression indeed. Fanny sighed and opened the drawing-room door.

Mamma and Mrs Robinson were seated on the sofa wearing their best clothes at each other. Mrs Robinson had the advantage of a very elaborate bonnet—a visit-paying bonnet—much decorated with ribbons and bows, and a pink silk parasol with artificial roses on it, and could therefore perhaps be said to have won. Mamma, on the other hand, was fighting back hard with her new sprigged muslin and a little muslin cap. They both had smiles fit to crack their faces.

"Ah," said Mrs Robinson, beaming, "and so here are dear Fanny and Emma and Albert and Harriet

and Charles and sweet little Jane and Susan."

"And there," said Mamma, beaming also, "are Violet and Harold and Gilbert and Louisa and dear little William and Eliza."

The Stanton children stood stock still in horror. For there, sitting in a row on the drawing-room chairs, also scrubbed, curled and buttoned into

Sunday clothes, were the invaders of Potter's Piece.
The two groups stared at each other, first in amazement and then with grim hostility. The Robinson
children were all very fair and pink-faced and gave a
most treacherous impression that butter wouldn't
melt in their mouths. The boys wore sailor suits and

pious expressions that changed to evil grins as soon as their mother wasn't looking. As for the girls, Fanny picked on Violet who seemed to be the eldest and realized that she had met the person she most disliked in the world. Hitherto, her best enemy had been Clara Binns the doctor's daughter. But now, studying Violet Robinson through narrowed eyes, it was as though Clara Binns had never existed. This was hate at first sight. Or rather second sight.

The Stantons said nothing. The Robinsons said nothing. Mamma and Mrs Robinson made polite conversation about health and weather and so forth. Tea was brought in by the maids and Fanny was obliged to watch the Robinsons take the largest and most inviting slices of cake. Potter's Piece was not mentioned, and the more it was not mentioned the more Fanny suspected that the Robinson children, like the Stantons, had good reason for not mentioning it. They too were not allowed out of their garden. She considered this, and saw that it might be a help.

The Robinsons made a great display of good manners. They pleased and thank you'd and the girls bobbed little curtseys to Mamma and the boys leapt up and down to pass the sugar and the muffins. Mrs Robinson looked smug and Mamma sat with a strained smile. Robinson behaviour, Fanny could see, was going to be held against the Stantons for some time to come. Once, when Mamma and Mrs Robinson were busy telling each other how delightful it would be for the children to have such charming neighbours, Fanny and Violet stuck their tongues out at each other.

"And the older children will be such company for each other in their lessons," went on Mrs Robinson. "It is so very good of you to have suggested it."

Fanny gaped. She saw the older Robinsons also look aghast. What was this? What appalling arrangement had been made behind their backs and over their heads? She turned to Mamma.

"Yes," said Mamma. "Mrs Robinson and I have a little surprise for you. Fanny and Albert and Emma are going to be joined at their lessons with Miss Purser by Violet and Harold and Gilbert. Is that not delightful?"

There was a shocked silence. "Every day?" said Fanny faintly.

Violet forgot herself so far as to say, "Oh, Mamma!"

"Every day," said Mamma sweetly. "And now I think it would be a nice idea, Fanny, if you were to take your new little friends up to see the schoolroom where they will be working."

Stantons and Robinsons climbed the stairs together. No one said a word. Outside the schoolroom Fanny paused, opened the door, and said to Violet with immense politeness, "After you." The Robinsons filed into the schoolroom, followed by the Stantons. Fanny closed the door.

And commotion broke out. Robinsons hurled insults at Stantons, who flung them back with gusto. The Young Children, in a fever of enjoyment and

excitement, shrieked and yelled and jumped about.
Albert tore off his jacket and squared his fists and
wanted to settle it then and there, once and for all,
taking on all the Robinson boys at once. Fanny and
Violet, older and wiser, restrained him. That way
lay disaster. Besides, it was a crude and wasteful way of

dealing with what looked like an interesting situation.

"It's ours!" said Fanny.

"It's no one's!" retorted a Robinson.

"It's ours more than it's anyone's!"

"Why?"

"Because we always go there."

"Well, we're going there now," said Violet.

A younger Robinson suggested that Potter's Piece be divided in two halves, the stream to form the dividing line, each family to occupy the half nearest their own garden.

For a moment Fanny considered this, until she saw the trap. On the far side of the stream, in what would under that arrangement be Robinson territory, was the chief attraction of Potter's Piece—the tumble-down pigsty which could be made into, depending on requirements, a native hut, a castle, a fortress, a house, or a stockade. Furthermore, the Robinsons would have the best climbing tree and the place where frogs came and the blackberry thicket and the swamp.

"If you promise not to go there again," she offered, with cunning, "we won't tell your Mamma you've been there."

There was a short silence. Then Violet countered, with a grin. "If you tell our Mamma we shall tell your Mamma you've been going there for years and years."

There could be no further negotiation. Everyone saw that. Only one thing was possible.

"War?" said Fanny, with a gleam in her eye.

"War to the bitter end," replied the Robinsons, with an answering gleam.

Then they got down to business. They sat round the enormous schoolroom table with its green baize ink-stained cover and drew up the rules of battle. Fanny fetched a sheet of paper from Miss Purser's desk and wrote at the top JUNE 8th 1866 DECLARATION OF WAR. She then made a careful list of names and ranks, on both sides. The Old Children were all to be Generals (thus avoiding any further arguments) and the Young Children were all to be infantry. Infantry might be taken prisoner, but must not be ill-treated and must be returned to their own side if weeping. Skirmishes and hand-to-hand fighting were only to take place between people of the same size. Full-scale engagements to include everyone. There was to be no throwing of anything that might actually cause damage, such as stones or sticks. Mud, if soft, was allowed. There was to be no biting, pulling of hair, or kicking. Pushing was acceptable. Territory occupied by four or more to be regarded as having fallen to the enemy, but might be recaptured at some future point. All fighting was to cease if either side had to withdraw owing to possible discovery by grown-ups, and the positions occupied at that moment were to hold until the next engagement.

They studied the document anxiously—at least those who could read did. Those who couldn't, such as William, Eliza, Charles, and Jane, pranced around the schoolroom excitedly. From time to time they showed unsuitable signs of friendliness towards the enemy and had to be pulled up sharply by their respective generals. When everyone was satisfied with the Declaration of War, the generals signed it in best handwriting. Then they all shook hands.

"Till tomorrow," said Violet solemnly.

"Till tomorrow," replied Fanny.

The next morning Fanny, Albert and Emma had breakfast in the nursery and then went downstairs for prayers, which they did every day. Papa and Mamma and the servants all assembled in the dining-room and Papa read a passage from the Bible and the children sat on uncomfortable chairs or knelt on the scratchy carpet. Opposite, the servants sat in a row: Cook and the two parlourmaids, and Nellie the kitchen maid. Sometimes prayers seemed to go on for ever. Fanny would sit in a daze, being only half awake at that time of day anyway, and Papa's voice would go on and on in the background like the wind on a stormy night or the noise of the sea, and shafts of light from the high windows would make rainbows on the floor and the table. And Fanny would squint at the rainbows through half-closed eyes and imagine herself floating on a cloud in heaven like the seraphim and cherubim of whom Papa was speaking. She tried to have nice thoughts during prayers, even if she wasn't listening properly; it seemed the least you could do. The trouble was, one thought led to another, so that you never knew where you might end up. Now, for instance, she began to wonder what sitting on a cloud felt like, and then how heavy seraphim were. Surely if they were at all heavy they would fall through, since clouds are thin airy things as you can see when the sun or the moon shines through them. And suppose one fell through, and landed in your own garden, and you found it there, complete with long white robe and harp and halo, how would you address it? Would the proper thing be to . . .

Albert gave her a nudge and she realized that the others were on their knees and prayers were coming to an end. "Amen," said Fanny, along with everyone else, and saw Cook heaving herself to her feet and giving her bad leg a rub. Cook and the maids filed off to the kitchen, Papa closed the Bible, checked the time on the gold watch that lived in his waistcoat pocket, as he did every day, and said to the children, "Off to your studies now, my dears," which he also did every day. They followed Miss Purser up to the schoolroom.

They were already settled round the green baize table when Violet and Gilbert and Harold arrived. Miss Purser made a great fuss of the visitors and a great performance of rearranging everyone. Fanny found herself sitting between Violet and Gilbert. They all three smiled sweetly until Miss Purser was busy at the blackboard writing down a list of words for spelling, and then they all pulled faces as hard as they could. Gilbert's angelic expression changed to a dreadful gargoyle grimace; even Fanny was impressed.

Miss Purser turned round and everyone composed themselves and began industriously scratching away at their slates.

The morning crept by like every schoolroom morning. They did spelling and sums and French verbs and more spelling and more sums and Fanny, Emma and Violet did needlework. Violet, Fanny noted, was as bad at sewing as she was herself. Curiously, this seemed a point in her favour. Violet's sampler, too, had got no further than the letters of the alphabet and the numbers one to ten. After that it was a sorry affair of unpicking and cobbling of mangled canvas and misplaced stitches wandering off in different directions. They sat side by side in a misery of pricked fingers and unthreadable needles, and felt something uncommonly like companionship in suffering.

At last it was dinner-time. "You may close your books," said Miss Purser, "and leave the room quietly. We shall see our little friends again to-morrow." She beamed upon Violet and Gilbert and Harold.

At the top of the stairs Stantons and Robinsons grinned evilly at each other in anticipation of the afternoon.

Never had dinner taken so long. Never had Nurse searched their plates with such an eagle eye, so that there was no way of hiding a single morsel under knife or spoon. And when at last they were allowed to leave the table, they must sit quietly and read an improving book while their dinners were digested. Fanny's improving book was about a girl who was so exquisitely behaved and charitable and self-sacrificing that everyone went around saying she was too good for this world, and sure enough by the fourth chapter she was dead of consumption, the fifth and final chapter being devoted to an enthusiastic description of her funeral. It made Fanny feel relieved that she was in no such danger herself, being full of faults, as Nurse and Miss Purser and Mamma and Papa were always pointing out.

At last they were released.

They pelted into the garden and off towards the lawn to the hedge—with a quick look round first to make sure no one was watching. Then through the hedge—generals first, with the infantry scuffling happily behind—and out into the long grass. "Ssh!" said Fanny. They lay in wary silence, peering down into Potter's Piece.

It was unnervingly quiet. Nothing moved. Birds flitted peaceably from bush to bush. The generals conferred, and decided the wise thing to do would be to send out a reconnaissance party; Albert wriggled out of the grass, crept away down the slope towards the stream and spotted, in the nick of time, the buttoned boot of an inadequately concealed Robinson sticking out from the elderberry thicket.

That was the glorious afternoon of the Ambush. And the Charge from the Blackberry Heights and the Skirmish by the Stream and the Fall of the Pigsty and

the Recapture of the Pigsty and the Retreat to the Spinney. There were full-scale engagements, when everybody on both sides rushed headlong across the grass, and stealthy outflanking manoeuvres ending with surprise attacks and resistances of incredible bravery. There were feats of heroism, such as Albert's rescue of Emma from the thorn tree in the face of overwhelming odds, and Gilbert's escape across the stream pursued by a horde of Stantons. Never had Potter's Piece seen such exploits. It was magnificent. Hours went by like minutes. With regret they heard the clock strike five. The generals ordered a cease-fire and immediate withdrawal for strategic reasons. It was tea-time. In acknowledgement of a well-ordered campaign, Robinsons cheered Stantons and Stantons cheered Robinsons.

Fanny, back in the garden, inspected her forces.

Everybody was filthy. Clothes were torn, hair-ribbons had been lost. The infantry, in particular, were in a deplorable state—mud from top to toe, and wildly over-excited. They retired behind the potting-shed to repair the worst of the damage before confronting Nurse.

It didn't help much.

If Miss Purser had not been so short-sighted, she might well have wondered, in the schoolroom next morning, why they all had a slightly battered appearance. Fanny wore a large bruise on the side of her face and Harold was a mass of blackberry scratches. Gilbert was limping. Emma had a cut on her hand which she proudly brandished at anyone who would look. There was an atmosphere of general high spirits, also ignored by Miss Purser, who was devoted this morning to writing appalling sums on the blackboard. The children stared gloomily at figures heaped in columns, figures snarling at each other in a network of multiplication signs and subtraction signs and addition signs, figures cowering inside brackets, figures capering away in thousands and tens of thousands and hundreds of thousands. Miss Purser scratched on, triumphant in a shower of chalk; the children sagged on to the schoolroom table, Miss Purser sat down and said smugly, "You may begin."

They wrote, they sighed, they writhed in anguish. They glared at the schoolroom clock, whose hand advanced by a minute in what must surely be half an hour. Fanny's head ached with the effort of trying to control all those fives and sevens and nines and twos which had a life of their own. As soon as she thought she had them where she wanted them they romped away, adding up different every time, tangling with one another till her head spun. Whatever were seven nines? She must have muttered it aloud, for an answering mutter came from Violet beside her, "Sixty-three."

"Thank you," whispered Fanny, and laboured on.

When at last the torment of arithmetic was over they did Scripture. They learned a psalm by heart, and repeated it verse by verse, taking it in turns. Then they did French verbs. "*J'aime, tu aimes, il aime . . .*" chanted Stantons, grinning menacingly at Robinsons.

"*Nous aimons, vous aimez, ils aiment*", responded Robinsons, threateningly. The hour of Potter's Piece drew nearer however much the clock might dawdle and loiter.

That was the afternoon of the Great Marsh Battle, when armies clashed in the boggy ground around the stream, when dripping Stantons were routed and driven up the hill towards the wall and rallied to come roaring down again with bloodcurdling yells. When Robinsons scattered and fled, only to rally and attack. When Stanton infantry, taken prisoner and imprisoned in the pigsty, escaped with amazing cunning through the unguarded window and were received back as heroes. When a Robinson general, surrounded in the spinney, broke through the enemy lines by wriggling snake-like through the undergrowth.

And when, in the heat of battle, the Stantons failed to hear Sukie calling them from beyond the garden wall, and were only saved by a message brought by a Robinson staff officer, who had keener ears. The Stanton high command sent a formal note of thanks for this piece of gentlemanly conduct on the part of the enemy.

There was terrible trouble with Nurse that afternoon, on account of mud and wetness and damage to pinafores and knickerbockers and stockings.

Next day the Robinsons reported trouble at their end too. In fact their Mamma had threatened that they should be confined to the house if they appeared in such a state again. The Stantons expressed sympathy. Though in that case, Fanny thought, we would have Potter's Piece to ourselves again. Curiously, this did not seem such an attractive idea after all.

The schoolroom morning proceeded according to pattern. There was a small diversion when Emma spilled her ink-well, sending a flood of ink across the already scarred and pock-marked table-cover. Emma had her knuckles rapped with Miss Purser's ruler; everybody, Robinsons included, glared resentfully at Miss Purser's back as soon as it was turned once more. Fanny, sunk in one of the deep, private trances that enabled her to get through the mornings, found herself with Miss Purser's beady eye upon her, and Miss Purser saying, "Fanny?" Something was expected, but what? The nine times table? The French verb 'to have'? The correct spelling of 'obedient'? She gazed at the ceiling, helplessly, and prayed for some kind of miracle.

"I wandered . . ." said Miss Purser, coldly, and for no apparent reason.

"I beg your pardon?" said Fanny, and felt a nudge from Violet. On Violet's slate had appeared a funny little drawing, some sort of flower. Now why ever. . . ?

"I'm waiting, Fanny," said Miss Purser.

A flower . . . what flower? The light dawned; of course—a daffodil! It was time for Recitation.

"I wandered lonely as a cloud
That floats on high o'er vales and hills,
When all at once I saw a crowd,
A host, of golden daffodils."

At the end of the morning Miss Purser said, "Now this afternoon, children, we are going to have an extra lesson."

Robinsons and Stantons looked at each other in consternation.

"We are going to go for a walk and do Nature Study," continued Miss Purser. "Put away your books, please, and leave the room quietly."

Gloomily they went downstairs.

After dinner they set off with Miss Purser, a reluctant procession. Fanny in particular was very contemptuous of the whole business. She herself was extremely interested in science—proper science, with Latin names for things and intense observation of the activities of creatures like caddis flies and spiders. Indeed, she had once found a fossil dinosaur, and was acquainted with a real member of the British Museum —but that is another story. Miss Purser's Nature Study, she knew from experience, was not going to be anything like that. Miss Purser was afraid of cows and disgusted by insects; in fact she hated Nature. Nature Study only happened two or three times a year when it was a nice day and Miss Purser felt like getting out of doors for a bit. And they might have been continuing the battle of Potter's Piece.

They trailed along. "Where are we going, Miss Purser?" asked Violet.

"Not very far," said Miss Purser. "There is a suitable place just by the garden, with abundant Nature." And she turned the corner off the road and down the little track that led to . . . Potter's Piece.

It was insult added to injury. How dare she! No grown-ups ever set foot in Potter's Piece; they had no right. United in outrage, Robinsons and Stantons plodded behind her exchanging bitter looks.

"You may gather wild flowers," said Miss Purser sitting down comfortably on a tree-stump, "and then we will see if we can name them. Be very careful not to get your feet wet or tear your clothes."

Sulkily, they dispersed over the grass. The familiar territory lay all round them—the slope, the blackberry bushes, the stream, the pigsty, the spinney—crying out to be put to proper use. They stumped about, and presently returned with mangled handfuls of flowers.

"Dandelion," said Miss Purser, peering. "Daisy. Buttercup. Er . . ."

"Meadow saxifrage," muttered Fanny, who knew about such things.

"Precisely," agreed Miss Purser, who did not, "and now I think we will go down to the stream and study the wonderful world of living creatures."

The wonderful world of living creatures included a fat frog sitting on a stone, deep in contemplation. Miss Purser gave a stifled scream. Fanny, who was fond of frogs, picked it up, very carefully so as not to hurt it, and they all gathered round to have a look at the frog's mysterious lidded eyes and huge gulping throat and delicate splayed hands. Except for Miss Purser, who retreated several yards and appeared much taken up with a clump of cowslips.

After that things improved somewhat. The children found various interestingly wriggly or multi-legged forms of life which they brought to Miss Purser, who was now looking rather pale and beginning to make remarks about the possibility of rain. A very large centipede, found under a stone by Gilbert, finally snuffed out Miss Purser's interest in the wonderful world of living creatures. She said hastily that it must be getting on for tea-time, and they must go back. On the way they would go through the spinney and listen to birdsongs.

Miss Purser set off in the direction of the spinney, lifting her skirts carefully to keep them clear of the damp grass. From time to time she called back warnings about nettles and thistles. The children, with a mixture of apprehension and interest, saw that she was heading straight for the marshy bit, an inviting stretch of bright green grass which in fact hid several inches of muddy water.

"Miss Purser . . ." Fanny began.

"Hush, Fanny," said Miss Purser, who was in the middle of a long and inaccurate account of bird migration. "I have told you many, many times not to interrupt."

Entranced, the children watched.

Miss Purser advanced into the bog, talking about our feathered friends. There was a squelching noise, a yelp of irritation, and Miss Purser became several inches shorter. There was a heaving and a floundering as she struggled to pull her boots clear of the mud.

"Oh, dear!" cried Fanny. "Poor Miss Purser, whatever shall we do!"

Spluttering noises from the rest were fortunately not heard by Miss Purser, who was now entirely taken up with her plight. The children raced round to the far side of the bog in time to receive her, sodden around the feet, her dress hemmed with mud, and extremely cross.

There would be no more Nature Study for quite a

while, Fanny suspected. The children escorted Miss Purser back to the house, trying hard to hide their gleeful smiles.

"That is a very disagreeable and dangerous place," said Miss Purser. "We shall not go there again." The children exchanged looks of satisfaction.

At lessons the next morning Miss Purser was shrouded in a thick shawl, declared herself to have a heavy cold, or worse, and sat for most of the time with her eyes closed wearing an expression of suffering.

After dinner Fanny led her troops down into Potter's Piece as usual. The Robinsons, she could see as they wriggled out of the hedge, were already there, sprawled around on the far side in rather unmilitary fashion.

"Shall we attack?" said Albert, half-heartedly.

Fanny looked across at the Robinsons, who were looking back. Indeed, a young Robinson had raised a hand and waved, in an equally informal way. She found suddenly that she wasn't at all sure that she felt like a battle, today. The Stantons also sat down on the grass. There was a nice smell of clover; bees were buzzing around and birds whistling away from the spinney.

Fanny made up her mind. "We'll ask for a cease-fire," she said. Adding hastily, "It doesn't mean of course the battle's *finished*, just we'll have a rest."

Albert, waving a white handkerchief tied to a stick as token of peaceful intent, crossed over the stream to the Robinsons. He returned to report that the suggestion of a cease-fire had been received with enthusiasm.

The two sides advanced slowly and met by the pigsty. After a moment Harold said thoughtfully, "What shall we do?"

One couldn't, after all, spend a cease-fire just sitting around doing nothing.

Harold went on, in an off-hand way, "Suppose we dammed the stream . . ."

Now curiously enough this was a project that the Stantons had often considered themselves, but somehow they had never got around to it in any serious way. An interesting and effective dam would involve hauling a lot of stones and sticks down to the stream, and with only three of you, at least three plus three Young Children who would only count as about one for dam-building purposes . . .

With six, on the other hand, plus three more Young ones . . .

"We are pioneer settlers in America," said Fanny happily. "We are clearing the forest before we build our hut and making a lake and the Young Children are Red Indians we have captured."

They set to enthusiastically. Stones and brushwood were brought down to the stream. Fanny and Violet took charge of the engineering strategy and directed operations. Once the Red Indians escaped into the spinney with much whooping and hilarity and had to be firmly suppressed. The dam grew, and a satisfactory if not very large lake began to form above it.

The lake was several inches deep in parts and most useful for cooling off during rest periods. They got even damper and muddier than during the most frenzied moments of warfare. The Red Indians lost interest and drifted off to build a wigwam of their own. The afternoon passed all too quickly. So quickly, indeed, that it was decided to extend the cease-fire into the next day.

But the Robinsons appeared to lessons in the morning with doleful faces. Their Mamma, they were able to whisper when Miss Purser's back was turned, had forbidden them to play out of doors for a whole week as a punishment for appearing in such a disgraceful state yesterday. The Stantons, who had endured a very sticky half hour with Nurse themselves and narrowly missed the same kind of sentence, expressed their sympathy.

"Anyway," said Albert, later, "we've got it to ourselves again now." He did not sound all that jubilant.

Fanny nodded.

That afternoon the Stantons returned to their old activities. They discovered the source of the Nile. They encountered and defeated a native tribe of incredible ferocity. They stalked a herd of buffalo. It was all quite agreeable. It passed the time. Somehow it lacked intensity.

The imprisoned Robinsons, the next day, hoped politely—and in tones of martyrdom—that the Stantons had had a pleasant afternoon.

And so it went on over the next few days. The Stantons did what they usually did at Potter's Piece, but the spice had gone out of things. On the fifth day they were slumped around on the grass after half an hour or so lacking inspiration and lacking leadership.

"What are we going to do now, Fanny?" said Emma, and Fanny lamely replied, after a minute or two, that she didn't know.

It was Harriet who put the unsayable into words. "It's better," she said, "when those other children are here. It's better than when it's just us." There was a long silence, as everyone digested this remark, and recognized the truth of it. The fact was, the battle of Potter's Piece had resulted in a situation that none of them would ever have guessed. Nobody had won and nobody had lost. In fact it had had the opposite effect to that usually expected of battles.

"Actually," said Harriet, airily, "I rather like the Robinsons."

And none of the others raised any objection.

That night, Fanny thought. If this was how things had turned out, well and good: everybody would be satisfied, and no hard feelings. On the other hand, Fanny liked to see things brought to their proper conclusion, and a battle does not just fizzle out, particularly so splendid a battle. It ends in victory or defeat: you know where you are. She lay in bed frowning into the heavily-breathing darkness of the nursery that she shared with Emma, Harriet and Jane, and arrived eventually at a most excellent solution. Then she went to sleep.

She and Albert drew up the Treaty. They drew it

up in red ink on a sheet of brown paper stolen from the pantry. Properly speaking, as they were well aware, the two sides should negotiate with each other before a Treaty is drawn up, but with the Robinsons confined to their house and Miss Purser's steely eye upon them all morning, there was really no way in which they could confer. The Stantons would just have to hope that the Robinsons would find the terms acceptable. Fanny rather thought they would, particularly when the second part of her plan was unfolded.

The Treaty when complete was very impressive. It positively dripped red ink and included a great many important-sounding words like 'hereinafter' and 'undersigned' and 'notwithstanding'. What it all added up to was that Robinsons and Stantons were to agree that the battle was at an end, with equal honours to both sides. Potter's Piece was to be common territory. Decisions about what they all did there were to be taken by everyone. And the signing of the Treaty was to be celebrated with a Banquet to be held in the pigsty. This last was Fanny's personal idea. Albert was full of admiration, though he had doubts about the details of the matter.

"How are we going to get food for a Banquet, Fanny?"

"I shall arrange it myself," said Fanny grandly.

On the day before the Robinsons were to be allowed out once more, Fanny and Albert smuggled the Treaty, rolled into a tube and sealed with a huge blob of red sealing-wax, into the schoolroom and handed it over under the table. Violet, looking a little mystified, received it and bore it away at the end of the morning.

The next day the Robinsons, with an air of friendly solemnity, brought it back, duly signed by all of them. Fortunately Miss Purser had one of her headaches, which meant that she had to leave the room from time to time for some fesh air, thus enabling the children to do some hasty planning.

I am afraid that some very unmilitary conduct took place that afternoon. In fact I suppose strictly speaking it was pilfering, if not downright theft, with bribery and corruption thrown in. Albert, who had an understanding with Nellie the kitchen maid, was able to make off with various small pies and other left-overs from the scullery behind Cook's back. Several Robinsons made a lightning raid on the store-cupboard and took over some biscuits and dried fruit that it seemed unlikely anyone would miss. Fanny and Violet, with permission, under the pretence of going for a walk together, went to the High Street where they visited the confectionery shop and spent all the pocket money that both families had been able to muster.

At three o'clock Robinsons and Stantons, each bearing a brimming basket, converged upon Potter's Piece.

And for the rest of the afternoon, in the seclusion of the pigsty, they celebrated the signing of the Treaty and the satisfactory conclusion of the battle for Potter's Piece. The infantry, I regret to say, all ate too much and ended up either asleep or feeling poorly. Fanny, Emma, Albert, Violet, Gilbert and Harold, having toasted each other in lemonade and eaten until they could eat no more, settled down to draw up their plans for the future maximum enjoyment of their afternoons.

A Selected List of Fiction from Mammoth

While every effort is made to keep prices low, it is sometimes necessary to increase prices at short notice. Mandarin Paperbacks reserves the right to show new retail prices on covers which may differ from those previously advertised in the text or elsewhere.

The prices shown below were correct at the time of going to press.

☐	7497 0978 2	**Trial of Anna Cotman**	Vivien Alcock	£2.50
☐	7497 0712 7	**Under the Enchanter**	Nina Beachcroft	£2.50
☐	7497 0106 4	**Rescuing Gloria**	Gillian Cross	£2.50
☐	7497 0035 1	**The Animals of Farthing Wood**	Colin Dann	£3.50
☐	7497 0613 9	**The Cuckoo Plant**	Adam Ford	£3.50
☐	7497 0443 8	**Fast From the Gate**	Michael Hardcastle	£1.99
☐	7497 0136 6	**I Am David**	Anne Holm	£2.99
☐	7497 0295 8	**First Term**	Mary Hooper	£2.99
☐	7497 0033 5	**Lives of Christopher Chant**	Diana Wynne Jones	£2.99
☐	7497 0601 5	**The Revenge of Samuel Stokes**	Penelope Lively	£2.99
☐	7497 0344 X	**The Haunting**	Margaret Mahy	£2.99
☐	7497 0537 X	**Why The Whales Came**	Michael Morpurgo	£2.99
☐	7497 0831 X	**The Snow Spider**	Jenny Nimmo	£2.99
☐	7497 0992 8	**My Friend Flicka**	Mary O'Hara	£2.99
☐	7497 0525 6	**The Message**	Judith O'Neill	£2.99
☐	7497 0410 1	**Space Demons**	Gillian Rubinstein	£2.50
☐	7497 0151 X	**The Flawed Glass**	Ian Strachan	£2.99

All these books are available at your bookshop or newsagent, or can be ordered direct from the publisher. Just tick the titles you want and fill in the form below.

Mandarin Paperbacks, Cash Sales Department, PO Box 11, Falmouth, Cornwall TR10 9EN.

Please send cheque or postal order, no currency, for purchase price quoted and allow the following for postage and packing:

UK including BFPO   £1.00 for the first book, 50p for the second and 30p for each additional book ordered to a maximum charge of £3.00.

Overseas including Eire   £2 for the first book, £1.00 for the second and 50p for each additional book thereafter.

NAME (Block letters) ....

ADDRESS ....

....

☐ I enclose my remittance for ....

☐ I wish to pay by Access/Visa Card Number

Expiry Date